SAVING SI

CW00868499

This Edition Published by Stanhope Books, Hertfordshire, UK 2022

www.stanhopebooks.com
Cover design and illustrations by Claudia Kirkby © 2021

ISBN-13: 978-1-909893-59-7

3

For Mum

loved more than words can say

And Dad

always missed – forever loved

ʌΛʌ

CONTENTS

PROLOGUE
AN EMOTIONAL DAY

The world is a beautiful place: whether it is a snow-capped mountain range or the sun setting over the sea, whilst sitting on a sandy beach; a bird singing in the trees or the first daffodil appearance of the spring. There is beauty everywhere.

For some, however, that is not always the case. For many the world can seem a sad, dark place - whether it be through poverty, ill health, abuse or loneliness. For some it is difficult to see the good. Sometimes you just have to look a little harder.

As Mary Bridges left Croydon, she was alone with her thoughts for the first time. It had been a difficult visit, with news she had not expected to hear, but she was glad she had made the effort to take the trip. As she drove south on the M23, en route back to Brighton, she thought back to the first time she had met Susan Sanderson. They had been eighteen years old and enrolled at university in Bournemouth to study English. Mary had little or no experience of the outside world and Susan seemed to be the only person who had taken a liking to her. They had not been great friends, with Mary liking her own space and company, but Susan was the closest anyone outside of home had come.

Mary had received a letter from Susan two weeks before, asking to see her. It was not the sort of thing Mary did lightly as the visit would take her out of her comfort zone. Especially a motorway drive to South London. The letter had been quite insistent and as Mary had not seen Susan for many years, she knew there had to be a valid reason for the request. She left everything at home in good hands and arrived in time for lunch.

Having been greeted warmly and hugged by her old friend, Susan had led Mary to the kitchen where they sat chatting happily and reminisced about their university days.

The two women enjoyed a tasty lunch and after Susan had cleared the table, Mary had bluntly asked why Susan had insisted on seeing her after so many years and having led such different lives. Unfortunately, the answer was neither what Mary expected or wanted to hear.

Susan explained she had something to tell Mary that she did not want her to hear any other way. She told that she had felt unwell for a while and, after a visit to the doctor and several tests, had been diagnosed with an inoperable brain tumour. Small, but none the less, deadly. And that she had been given just a few weeks, or maybe a couple of months at best, to live.

The announcement had hit Mary like a bolt of lightning, and as she rethought the conversation a tear rolled down her cheek. It had been shocking news: something that no one ever wanted to hear from a friend or relation; and what had amazed Mary the most was how well Susan had looked. She loved her job and her pet cat, Rufus, and had never looked so healthy. Ironic really, Mary thought, as she brushed away the tear, wondering if she would ever see Susan again.

Bringing her attention back to her driving, trying to concentrate on the busy motorway, Mary realised she had just passed the exit to Gatwick Airport and knew she would arrive back in about an hour. At that moment, a large British Airways aeroplane flew across the motorway directly in front of her car. It took her by surprise, how low it was flying, and she hoped it would make a safe landing at the airport. Suddenly, it brought another image to Mary's mind which caused her to forget all about Susan.

A picture of a small plane crashing into a mountain flashed before her eyes, causing her to swerve the car onto the hard shoulder and almost come to a stop. Her heart was pounding, and she could feel sweat on her forehead as she tried to compose herself and continue her journey. It was a frightening image, one that Mary had not experienced before, although it was a scenario she knew well.

Ever since Mary had been a small child, she had seen things she could not explain. A bloodied face, a car crash or a collapsed building. Sometimes the visions were a very quick flash, like the one that had just occurred, and sometimes a full-blown, series of events almost like a full-colour, mini movie. She had no control over it and had no answers as to why it happened. But one thing she did know, was that it was not good news.

As Mary grew the visions decreased and now, for reasons she could not explain, they had returned. First there had been the avalanche, then the prison cell, and now this.

Feeling unnerved, Mary tried to forget the terrible image of the plane crash. It had been a long, tiring and emotional day, and when she arrived home, she promised herself she would have a relaxing hot bath. First though, she would watch the news to make sure that no plane crash had occurred that day. Finally, she would have an early night, happy to be back in her home. The home she had known all her life and adored.

CHAPTER ONE
WEIRD OR WONDERFUL

"Stop doing that. You're freaking me out," Moose shouted at Reggie, as his pen smoothly rolled forward and back on the table in front of them, all of its own accord.

"What?" Reggie replied. "I don't get your problem; I'm only looking at it. It if wants to roll around then I don't know what I can do about it."

"I'll tell you what you can do about it. You can stop looking at it and casting a spell or whatever strange thing you do to make it move," Moose hissed.

"Will you two please stop the arguing? Moose leave him alone; he is not hurting you." Seamus interrupted to try and stop the bickering between the other two boys.

"Well, you would say that wouldn't you? What would you know any way? You can't even see what he is doing," Moose said turning his anger toward Seamus.

"Really uncalled for Moose," Reggie clenched his fists, ready to protect his friend.

"Ah, the two little love birds sticking up for each other," Moose seemed to be acting extra mean today for some reason.

"Oh, just shut up," Seamus told him, trying to get him to back off. "You'd better be quiet now; I can hear Mother coming."

"Yes, of course you can. You and your super hearing. Strange no one else can hear her," Moose continued. "God, you two are so weird, I don't get you at all."

"You do not get what, Moose?" Mary, known to the children as Mother, asked as she walked in the door of the lounge.

Mary was the owner of this place they all called home. Her home, their home. The home she had known all her life. When Mary was a child, she had come to live in the large house in Brighton that was then an orphanage. She had no parents that she could remember and had no memories of anything before the orphanage. The only person that had ever resembled a mother was Mrs Hawthorn, the lady who owned and ran the place back then.

Mary had arrived in 1967, when she was just a few months old, and dear Mrs Hawthorn had loved her and brought her up as her own. She said that Mary always seemed to have that something a little more special than the rest of the children. And, over the years, as the other children came and went, Mary stayed forever. She had been home schooled, with the orphanage being all she knew and all she wanted to know.

As she grew, Mary developed a knack for seeing strange things happen in her mind and Mrs Hawthorn always put it down to an overactive imagination; but Mary knew better. Whenever she had a vision or insight, she could always guarantee that within the next couple of days, she would see something on the television or read something in the newspaper that indicated her vision had happened somewhere in the world. It seemed very strange to Mary, and it had frightened her to think that maybe her visions were causing these terrible incidents to happen. So, she kept them to herself and tried very hard to dismiss them from her head. And sure enough, as she grew into her teenage years, the visions occurred less and less.

When Mary turned eighteen, Mrs Hawthorn sent her off to university to get a degree and hoped that she would fall in love with the outside world and find a new life for herself. That, however, never happened. Mary's life was the orphanage and after three years, English degree in hand, she returned, as if she had never been away.

Unfortunately, on her return Mary found that Mrs Hawthorn had grown old and frail in the years she had been gone, caused by the stress of looking after the orphanage on her own. Mary did all she could to take the pressure off Mrs Hawthorn, but sadly the old lady passed away a few months after Mary came back. It was the first huge moment of anguish in Mary's life, and she grieved for the woman she loved so much.

On the day of her funeral, a letter arrived from the council, addressed to Mrs Hawthorn. Mary opened it, making a note to inform them of her passing. As she read, she discovered that new laws had been passed about children living in care and that orphanages across the country were being phased out and the children to be found new homes in the community.

As if that day had not been bad enough burying her 'mother', now Mary had to deal with the idea of the orphanage closing too. She tried to go about her normal duties without causing alarm to the children still in residence there. She loved them all and worried about where they would end up, and where she would go once the orphanage was closed. But she did not have to wait too long. For a week after Mrs Hawthorn's funeral, her solicitor came to see Mary and informed her that the old lady had left her the whole estate. The money, the land and, most importantly to Mary, the orphanage. It was all hers, every last brick.

Learning this gave Mary a new view on life and made her determined not to lose the children who lived there. She told the council that she now owned the property and applied to be a foster parent, knowing that by doing so she could keep the house open, providing them all with a home until they were either adopted, fostered by another family, or old enough to leave.

Calling the home Hawthorns Home for Foundling Children in memory of her late guardian, things got back to normal, and everyone was very happy living with Mary. She was a wonderful teacher and role model to them all and they loved her very much. Some of the children that had been there for a very long time knew little or nothing of their biological parents, and as Mary had once referred to Mrs Hawthorn, they now called her Mother.

"Oh, nothing, just having a bit of fun with the guys, you know," Moose replied trying to make light of the situation.

"Yes, Moose, I can imagine you having a lot of fun at the expense of Reggie and Seamus. Just behave yourself for once in your life, can't you?" Mary snapped.

Moose Higginbottom was a round, burly chap who had come to Hawthorns from an assortment of four different foster homes in the last five years. He was fourteen years old and had never really been given a fair chance at life. He behaved badly, took umbrage to discipline and was always in the thick of any trouble brewing.

"Are you okay, Mother?" Reggie asked, noticing the sharp tone to her voice that was not normally there. "How was your trip to London yesterday?"

"Yes, Reggie, I'm fine. Thank you for asking. I think I'm just a little tired from the long drive." The boys sensed something was not right as she was not usually short with them. "It was nice to see my old friend, but unfortunately she is rather unwell, and I guess I am a little worried about her."

"If we can do anything to help, Mother, you will ask, won't you?" Seamus offered.

"Yes thank you, Seamus, I know. But there is very little anyone can do it seems. Just please behave yourselves," she said glaring directly at Moose as she left the room.

"You are such a goodie-goodie," Moose spoke to Seamus as soon as the door to the lounge was closed. "If we can do anything to help... blah blah blah."

"Oh, shut up, Higginbottom. It wouldn't hurt you to be a little nicer from time to time," Reggie said staring at a book on the occasional table near to where Moose stood.

17

A second later the book rose up from the table, flew towards Moose and hit him sharply on the side of the head, before falling to the floor.

"Ouch, that really hurt," Moose squealed rubbing his temple. "I'll get you for that when you are least expecting it. Just you wait and see," he said, still holding his sore head as he opened the lounge door to leave.

"That's it. Go on, run away," Seamus said laughing at what he had heard.

"Seriously, Reggie, keep your eyes open 'cause your mate there can't. I will get you back for that. You really are a couple of weirdos." Moose was seething as he left the room and slammed the door behind him.

"That was wonderful, Reg, well done. I guess it was a book that hit him. It must have really hurt. Wonderful, really wonderful," Seamus told his friend, beginning to relax now that Moose had left the room.

Seamus O'Donnell was twelve years old and had arrived at Hawthorns just six months before. His parents had both died in a car accident on a rural country lane near his old home in Southern Ireland when he was only nine years old. Shortly after their deaths he had moved to Hastings to live with his gran who was his only remaining relative. It had been a difficult existence for a young boy with a disability, and his grandmother had done her best by him. Sadly, she too had died leaving him alone in the world, until he came to live with Mary at Hawthorns.

For Seamus, the world was a dark place due to a severe lack of vision. Before he was born, he had contracted the chicken pox virus from his pregnant mother, and shortly after his birth his parents had been informed by doctors that he was blind. As he grew, they discovered he was able to see shadows, the outlines of large shapes, and that he could differentiate between light and dark. It seemed a very sad way for a young boy to live his life, but Seamus never complained. He was a happy child and made up for his disability in other ways. When he was five years old and had been walking through the countryside with his mother and the family dog, the dog had escaped the confines of its lead and ran from the field into the road. His mum had quickly run after the dog and as she reached the road, Seamus heard the engine of a car approaching from along the lane. His mother had not heard the car, but thanks to Seamus alerting her, she managed to pick up the dog and jump to safety as it appeared from around the bend.

After that, his parents had taken him to the hospital where many tests had been performed on his hearing. It had astounded doctors to admit that Seamus had an audible capability greater than any person they had ever come across. The doctors did explain that sometimes when one sense is lost another may become heightened, but Seamus took that theory to a whole new level.

In his few short months at Hawthorns, Seamus found a new happiness that he had not had for a long time. He became an instant best friend to Reggie and loved Mary in the same way he had loved his own mother. Reggie was very happy to have him there too, as he now had an ally in his spats with Moose.

"Do you think I'm weird, Seamus?" Reggie asked his friend now they had the room to themselves. "I totally get that it's not normal that I can move stuff around, and that other kids can't do it, but it just happens so easily. What do you think?"

"No, Reggie, I don't think you are weird. Yes, it may be a little unusual but that makes you special in my book. I think you are wonderful," Seamus told his best friend.

CHAPTER TWO
D-VISION

Life was good at Hawthorns and all ten of the children that occupied the rooms of the swamping three storey townhouse were very happy. Many of them had received a tough start in life and Mother Mary made it her aim to provide them all with the love, security and education they needed. They were all home schooled and she made sure that each one of them worked as hard as they could to achieve good grades.

Of course, Mary could not have coped with three teenagers and seven younger children on her own, and the law would not have allowed her to. So, she had been very thankful when Sister Alice Gilligan had come to live at Hawthorns five years before. She came from a small remote convent in Southern Ireland when her order had closed. She loved her new position, always believing that working in the community with children had been her real calling. For Mary she was a welcome extra pair of hands and the two women worked well together. And, with the added help of a cook and a cleaner who came in for a couple of hours every day, they had become close friends and Hawthorns ran like clockwork.

Sister Alice had been a big hit with the children too. Because of her lack of experience in the real world they loved to teach her about music, fashion and anything else that was important to them. Alice also loved to learn all they had to offer. There was one girl, however, that she enjoyed spending time with the most.

When Sister Alice arrived at Hawthorns, she'd met five-year-old Jasmin Dharlia, who was now ten and had been in residence the longest. Sister Alice knew it was not right to have a favourite, but it was difficult not to. Jasmin was the most beautiful child, with large black eyes, olive skin and long, glossy black hair. She was also the most loving and most intelligent child. She had an IQ of one hundred and forty-five and was an incredible mathematician. She often studied on her own until Mary procured a local, retired university lecturer to come and work with her. There was not an equation or problem that she could not solve; and not a puzzle, code or combination that she could not crack.

On the morning Jasmin arrived at Hawthorns, Mother Mary had been alerted to a crying sound outside the front door and, upon investigation, discovered a tiny baby wrapped in a woollen shawl. She had looked everywhere, to no avail, for the infant's mother and on alerting the authorities, they concluded that Jasmin could stay at Hawthorns until her parents were found – and she had been there ever since. Mary was later informed that her parents had both come from India as teenagers to train as doctors at the local university. They had met and fallen madly in love. A few months later Jasmin's mother had found herself pregnant and on telling her boyfriend of the happy upcoming event, he had hung himself from fear of the shame it would bring on his family. Having spent a long and lonely pregnancy, grieving for her soul mate, Jasmin's mother made the decision that she could not continue to live without him. At just a few days old, she left Jasmin on the steps of Hawthorns, and in the identical manner as her beloved, had taken her own life.

It was saddest story Mary had ever heard, and she committed to making Jasmin's life the best she could. She had fostered her and given her all the care she needed. And now with Sister Alice doting on her too, Jasmin was a happy and well-loved child.

On the day of Jasmin's fifth birthday, Mary responded to a loud hammering on the front door and was greeted by a dishevelled looking woman and a sweet, blonde haired child. The woman had pushed her way past Mary into the hallway, dragging the young girl by the hand behind her.

"This is Paxton Day, my daughter. She is eight, and I need you to take her off my hands," the angry faced woman told Mary. "She is a devil and has caused nothin' but trouble for me and my fella. I can't deal with her anymore; so, she's yours now. Do what you want with her."

Mary had remembered staring at the bolshy woman and then at the cute girl and wondered how this woman could say these things about her own daughter. What on earth could she have done at eight years old that was so terrible?

"I'm sorry, Mrs Day," Mary tried to tell her. "I can't just take your child, there are procedures to follow. If you contact the authorities, perhaps they can help."

"Authorities, rubbish! What do they know?" You're 'n home, ain't you? One that looks after children?" The awful woman demanded to know.

"Well, yes, but it's not that simple, I'm afraid, you have to...." Mary tried to explain.

"I don't have to do nothing, she's your responsibility now. I want nothing more to do with her. Evil brat!" And with that she had turned and walked out the door leaving Mary and Paxton stunned.

Mary had taken Paxton into the birthday party they were holding for Jasmin. It was the first birthday party Paxton had ever been to, and as she sat shyly in the corner, Jasmin walked over to her and offered her a piece of birthday cake. Slowly but surely a smile appeared on Paxton's face, and from that moment on the two girls had been like sisters.

As Paxton grew used to everyone at Hawthorns, she came out of her shell little by little, but always remained shy and introvert. She had told Mary that her life with her birth mother and stepfather had been so awful she was glad her mother had given her up. She had never known her real father and her mother had remarried a dreadful man when Paxton was three years old. She told a tale of violence and abuse that she had suffered at his hands, and how she had run away several times. Each time being found by the police, just to be returned to suffer more degradation. Finally, when a teacher at school noticed some bruises on her neck, Paxton had been encouraged to speak out about her stepfather, and after a long and upsetting court case, he had been sentenced to ten years in prison. At last, the physical abuse had ended, but the emotional abuse from her mother became worse than ever. She had never believed a word Paxton said about her husband and blamed her daughter for his imprisonment; until one afternoon she told Paxton they were going to visit a friend and ended up on the doorstep of Hawthorns.

Everyone who met Paxton acknowledged that she was a joy to be around, and when they learned her story, they could not believe how anyone could treat another human being so badly. All except one. One of the other girls, Prudence Spragg, was the same age as Paxton and had arrived at Hawthorns not long after. She was clearly jealous of the attention Paxton received and could be quite cruel. Paxton had a lot of support from the other children, so Prudence had to be quite careful not to push her luck. Until the day Moose Higginbottom came to live with them.

Prudence and Moose had a lot in common, both being passed around from one foster family to another, and she quickly became accomplice and wing-man to his antics.

When Moose first arrived, Prudence had convinced him to lock Paxton in the garden greenhouse. She had not meant to do her any harm. She just wanted to get her out of the way for a while. Sadly, the confinement reminded Paxton of when her stepfather used to lock her bedroom door. She had called for help, but with no response to her cries, she quickly began to panic. Stress and fear rose inside her, and feeling she would never be freed, let out a loud scream. She was not prepared for what happened next and quickly fell to the floor to shield her face and head as the panes of glass around her began to shatter and crash to the ground. Thankfully, she had not been badly hurt, although it had been a terrifying ordeal. And one for which Moose and Prudence had been severely punished.

After that day, the abuse and torment that Moose and Prudence dished out was less sinister, as all the other children did their best to shield Paxton, knowing she was the last person that deserved their nonsense.

One evening, soon after the incident, some of the children sat in the library reading, when Prudence entered and headed straight towards Paxton. "What rubbish are you reading?" she said, wrenching the book from Paxton's hands and flicking through the pages.

"It's mine, give it back," Paxton pleaded, not wanting to get into an argument.

"Not until you tell me what it's about. Looks really dull to me, lots of silly pictures," Prudence taunted.

"It's a book that Sister Alice lent me to read. It's about mountain ranges across the world and the hidden civilisations that live in them. Apparently, there is a place in the Himalayas in South Asia called Shangri La that no one has ever found," Paxton told her with great interest.

"How boring. Sounds like rubbish to me. There are far better things to be interested in than that," Prudence replied, still not handing the book back.

Standing up from the chair where he had been watching patiently Reggie moved close to Prudence and told her to give the book back.

"It's all right, Reggie, Prudence can look at it if she wants to." Paxton didn't want any trouble.

"No, she can't. It belongs to Sister Alice, and she gave it to you to read, not her," he replied. "Now Spraggs, give it back before I get mad, and then run along and find your play mate," he said, referring to Moose.

"Okay, have it your way, tough guy," Prudence backed down as she threw the book into Paxton's lap. "If you like the Himalaya thingies so much why don't you do us a favour and shove off over there and leave us all alone? Guess I'll see you all later. Happy reading!" she remarked sarcastically as she left the room.

Paxton smiled at Reggie and said, "Thanks, Reggie, that was kind of you. I love that you always have my back." And he did.

Reggie Davenport was the oldest of the ten children at Hawthorns, preceding Moose by three months which pleased him immensely. He had only been there for two years, but he had quickly found his place and became the silent guardian of all the younger children. He was a strong minded yet tender chap and was not going to put up with any nonsense from Moose or Prudence.

He was born and raised in Brighton, so was a local lad and used to walk past Hawthorns on his way to school every day never dreaming that he would end up living there. His upbringing had been one of privilege compared to all the other children, having attended a private school and holidaying all over the world. His parents had been good to him, giving him everything he wanted materially, but he always felt something was missing. They seemed happier to leave him with a nanny to attend social gatherings and functions rather than spending time with him.

Thankfully, he had a good relationship with his nanny and as small boy had liked to play tricks on her by hiding or moving things around their house. One day she had promised to take him to the park, but his parents came home early and said he had to go out with them. Preferring to walk to the park with his nanny, Reggie thought about hiding his father's car keys so they could not leave the house. As he thought about where to hide them, he watched the bunch of keys slide off the hall console table and onto the floor. He realised it was a strange thing to happen, and as he thought about picking them up, the keys lifted off the floor and landed back on the table.

It was the first time anything like that had happened, and Reggie had to admit he was rather freaked out by it. Before long, however, he mastered his ability and had things moving about all over the place. It was an incredibly odd thing to be able to do, but Reggie revelled in his newly found form of sorcery.

Unfortunately for Reggie, when he was twelve, disaster struck and there was nothing neither he nor his magic could do about it. He remembered being called to the Head Teacher's office one afternoon at school to find two police officers and his aunt from London in the room. He didn't recall much about the meeting other than the words, parents, skiing, accident and dead. In the space of a few seconds, he had been made an orphan and his world ripped apart. And to make matters worse his only living relative, his aunt, declared that she would not give him a home.

Having made arrangements for him to move in with Mary, his aunt very swiftly made her way back to her fancy property in Chelsea, West London and Reggie had never heard a word from her since.

As with all the other children, he was happy at Hawthorns, although he still missed his parents and the life they had lived and knew he always would. Sometimes at night he would lay wide awake staring at the ceiling of his room wondering if the power he had been given was some sort of punishment. He would have gladly lost his special ability if it meant getting his parents back.

He said as much to Paxton one day when they sat in the garden together and she assured him that he had been given his gift for a reason. She also felt sure that one day he would get the opportunity to put it to good use.

Having thought seriously about what Paxton had said, Reggie knew that it made sense, and at that moment he realised that his three closest friends at Hawthorns all had special talents too.

"I have the most wonderful idea," he told Seamus, Paxton and Jasmin when he gathered them together after dinner that evening. "I have given a lot of thought to the strange things that we can do. Seamus your supersonic hearing, Pax your ability to scream at such high decibels you can shatter glass, and you, little Jasmin, with your magnificent brain, the four of us could be invincible."

"Yes, so what are you getting at?" Seamus queried.

"A secret club just for the four of us," Reggie continued.

"Sounds cool," Paxton said. "We will need a name though."

"I have thought of that too," Reggie told his three friends. "Knowing what we can all do, I realised that maybe we have been brought together for a reason. I thought about a sort of military name like squad or battalion, somehow using our surnames, Davenport, Dharlia, Day and O'Donnell. Then Mother Mary's visions popped into my head. And it hit me. So, ladies and gents, drum roll please. I give you D-vision. What do you think? Are you in?"

"Oh yes, Reggie, definitely. We're in," Seamus, Paxton and Jasmin replied in unison.

CHAPTER THREE
THREE LETTERS

Summer was in full swing, and everyone at Hawthorns was happy and content. They enjoyed long warm days, playing football and rounders in the garden and eating numerous barbecues. Much to the delight of all the children, Moose and Prudence had not been too unbearable to live with, and Mary and Sister Alice delighted in the peace and quiet. Reggie and Seamus had built a tree house for all the kids to use, although obviously, Seamus could not do any of the building, but he had helped Reggie with gathering tools and equipment. When it was finished Paxton and Jasmin had made pretty curtains for the window and Sister Alice had given them an old rug from her bedroom for the floor. They held an official opening ceremony with lemonade and cupcakes, and Reggie declared it the official D-vision meeting place.

Sister Alice had kept a close eye on Seamus when he was carrying the tools that Reggie needed and gave him as much help as she could. As well as her soft spot for Jasmin she also felt a special fondness for Seamus. She had known him in his hometown in Ireland when he was just a small boy. Before his parents died, she had taught some lessons at the special needs school he attended and had liked him immediately.   He was a warm, thoughtful boy and she had been devasted when she heard the news of his loss. Therefore, now they were living under the same roof she wanted to make his life as easy as possible.

One morning when all the children were eating breakfast, Sister Alice entered the dining room and handed Mary the morning post that had just arrived.   Mary studied the official looking envelope and recognised the mark in the top left-hand corner. She knew it was the logo of her bank and excused herself.

"Is everything okay, Mary?" Sister Alice asked, seeing a strange look on her friend's face.

"Yes, just a letter from the bank. I don't know why they are writing to me, but I'm sure it's nothing. I'll read it in the study."

Once in the privacy of her office, Mary used her letter opener to tear through the top of the envelope and remove the letter.

Dear Miss Bridges,

It has come to our notice that in recent months your business account has reached the maximum of lending and that you have, on several occasions, exceeded your top overdraft limit, causing unofficial borrowing.

We are aware that since commencing your business you have been in difficulty at various times, and we do endeavour to help our customers to the best of our ability.

However, unfortunately at this time, with the lack of funds entering your account, the bank feels that we must ask you to pay back the balance of the loan at your earliest convenience.

Please do not hesitate to contact me if you have any questions or require further assistance.

Yours sincerely,

Mr Albert Pennygrabber
Assistant Manager, Bank of Brighton

Mary stood speechless, staring at the piece of paper in her hand. How could this have happened? She knew that things had been tight recently. Government funding had been cut back and charitable donations were thin and far between, but she never dreamt she had let things get so bad.

There was a gentle tap on the door. It opened and Sister Alice popped her head in.

"The children have gone to wash up and prepare for lessons. Anything else you would like me to do?" She had a gut instinct that something was wrong and wanted to offer any assistance she could.

Mary, still feeling the shock of what she had just read, handed the letter to Alice, who quickly skimmed over the printed lines of text, and gasped as she reached its conclusion.

"Oh, my blessed father!" Sister Alice exclaimed as she handed the letter back to Mary. "What on earth does it mean?"

"Well, I'm afraid it means we are broke. When I inherited the house, I had a small monetary bequest from Mrs Hawthorn but that has long gone. With no income, I relied on grants and contributions, although they were never enough for us all to live on. So, I took a loan from the bank, and now it seems they wish me to repay it. I had no idea that I had got so far into debt. What will I tell the children?" Mary looked devastated.

"So, what will you do?"

"I will have to give it some thought Alice, but as it stands, the only way I possibly have of paying them back …. is to sell the house," Mary said sadly. "I don't see any other way."

As promised Mary gave the situation a lot of thought in the coming days and spoke to the bank to see if she could pay the loan back gradually, but with no regular income they were not satisfied that she would be able to keep up with the repayments. So, as far as they were concerned nothing would change. And, as for endeavouring to help their customers, they offered no help at all. They wanted their money back and that was that.

A week after the letter arrived, and seven sleepless nights trying to think of an alternative solution, Mary gathered all ten children, along with Sister Alice, the cook and the housekeeper into the lounge after breakfast. Everyone could see from her exhausted face that something was wrong, and she had been quieter than usual for several days. She did not know how to tell them but knew she could not dress it up. She had to be honest. She began with telling them about the letter from the bank and what it meant financially.

"So, how will we get enough money to pay it back?" Mary loved the way Reggie used the term 'we' as if it were the responsibility of all of them to muck in.

"That is just it," she told everyone gathered. "I have done the sums, and whatever I do I cannot raise the money required or pay back any further instalments. I'm afraid, and it breaks my heart to say it, but I think I am going to have to sell this house."

"You can't!" Jasmin shouted. "It is my home. I have never known anything else. You are my family. What will happen to us?" Tears began to roll down her cheeks and she began to shake uncontrollably.

Reggie moved close to her and wrapped his arm around her shoulders to comfort her, as the rest of the children began to bombard Mary with a barrage of questions.

"Listen to me, please." She wanted to restore order in the room so she could talk to the children as calmly as possible. "I am sorrier than I can say, but I am going to have to find new foster homes for all of you. There is no way I can afford to keep any of you with me."

Mary felt her heart breaking as she spoke the words. Tears gushed from her eyes and everyone in the room sat in stunned silence. She promised she would find a wonderful home for each of them and that the bank had confirmed she could stay in the house until all the children had been rehomed.

It was the most devastating thing to have happened to them since the terrible situations that had brought them all together. They loved Mother Mary and Sister Alice, yet more importantly they felt secure and safe, and it worried them all that they may never find that again.

The atmosphere at Hawthorns changed that day; the girls cried a lot and the boys seemed angry all the time. The cook and the housekeeper had promised to work for nothing until Mary needed to let them go, which was a weight off her mind. Sadly, now though, all she could think about was the children. She sat up most nights researching families and other private homes like hers and spent her days making telephone calls to everyone possible. It was the hardest and most upsetting time of her life, nevertheless it had to be done. She had to remain strong.

Two long weeks later, she had found homes for four of the children, but Moose, Prudence and D-vision were proving much harder. It had not been difficult to find foster homes for the youngest children, with the hope that they would all be adopted. It was the older children that were far from easy to rehome.

"Just one letter this morning, Mary," Sister Alice said, entering the study and finding Mary behind her desk on the phone, as was usual these days.

She indicated to Alice to place the letter down on the desk and gave her a thumbs-up in thanks for bringing it in. Like everyone in the house, Alice was also devastated at the thought of leaving Hawthorns. She would probably be shipped back to a convert somewhere in Ireland, although she really did not want to be parted from the children. To Mary she had been a rock and wonderful companion, and it was breaking them all inside that very soon it would come to an end.

As Mary replaced the telephone receiver, she picked up the letter in front of her and opened the handwritten envelope with her faithful old letter opener. She did not recognise the handwriting but knew who it was from the moment she started to read.

Dear Mary,

It is with great sadness that I write to you today to inform you of the passing of our beloved Susan. She left her father and I four days ago after a prolonged spell in hospital. We had hoped to bring her home at the end but unfortunately, she was taken too quickly. Perhaps a blessing some might say.

I wanted to write to you as soon as I could. Susan always spoke very highly of you, and I wanted to thank you for being a good friend to her over the years. She told us recently how much your last visit had meant to her and how much she enjoyed seeing you.

The funeral will be held on Friday 30th September at the Sutton Crematorium at 3.00pm. We would be delighted to see you and it would be a great honour if you could perhaps prepare a reading to be given on the day.

With thanks and we look forward to seeing you on the 30th.

Warmest regards,

Mrs June Sanderson

As she folded the letter and put it in her pocket, Mary realised she was crying again. She had done a lot of that recently and wondered when things would improve. It was turning out to be an emotionally tough period in her life, and now the sad news of her friend passing added to her distress. She gave a thought to how June, Susan's mum and Stan, her father must be feeling. To lose a child is said to be the hardest thing that any parent can go through, and the only way that Mary could liken it to her current situation, was that she felt like she was losing ten of her own.

She made a note in her diary of the funeral date and knew that she could not refuse Susan's parents by saying a few words on the day. She sat staring into space thinking about their days at university and what she might like to say about Susan and didn't emerge from her office for a couple of hours. She thought about the last time she had seen Susan and realised that she had outlived the doctor's timeline by nearly a month, which was testament to her determination. It made Mary doubly glad she had gone to visit her, especially as it had been such a long drive. And then she remembered the journey home. With everything that had happened she had forgotten about her vision of the crashing aeroplane; and having seen nothing on the news about an actual incident happening, had put it down to her imagination.

When she did finally make an appearance, Sister Alice and the children had just entered the dining room for lunch.

"Are you all right, Mother Mary?" Jasmin asked, noticing her red eyes and nose.

"Yes, thank you, Jasmin. I'm fine. I just had some bad news, that's all." More bad news, she wanted to say but didn't.

"Goodness, you look terrible, Mary. What has happened?" Sister Alice could see instantly that she had been crying.

"You remember I told you about my friend Susan, who I visited in London at the start of the summer? The letter you brought me in earlier was from her mother. She passed away a few days ago," Mary told her friend in a hushed voice not wanting the children to hear.

"Oh, bless my soul, you poor lamb, you must feel terrible. Is there anything I can do for you?" Sister Alice put an arm around Mary to console her as the two ladies sat down to eat.

"No, thank you, Alice, you have been magnificent taking the brunt of running this place for the last couple of weeks. I am fine, really. It is such a shame when people are taken so young. I will always remember her with fondness, but my aim now is to find homes for the rest of the children, get this place sold and get the bank off my back."

"Well, Mary, if anyone can do it you can," Sister Alice had so much faith in her. "Just let me know whatever you need, and I will do my best to make your life as easy as possible."

"I know you will, Alice, thank you!"

The next morning Mary received a telephone call from a lady in Hastings who had a large house and fostered as many children as she could to fill it. She told Mary that she had room for two children and that she especially liked to help children with behavioural issues. That was music to Mary's ears and from what she learnt, she knew the position would be perfect for Moose and Prudence. They would flourish in the environment that had been set out to her and as they got along so well, Mary believed that keeping them together would benefit them both.

When she told the pair, they took the news well and were grateful to Mary for keeping them together. Hastings was not too far away, and from what they had heard about the house, it seemed very similar to the Hawthorns they knew and loved. It would be a massive change, of course, but felt certain they would soon get themselves noticed and fit right in.

"Funny isn't it, how you four are the only ones left that Mother Mary hasn't been able to find a home for," Moose goaded Reggie, Seamus, Paxton and Jasmin. "Guess no one wants to give a home to your silly little gang. Mind you the chances of you being kept together are non-existent so your gang will be defunct. Ah, what a shame!"

"I think you'd better shut up, Moose, you are upsetting the girls." He and Reggie always seemed to be at loggerheads these days.

"Oh yes, we can't upset the girls can we? I'm not surprised though, who would want four freaks like you anyway? With all your strange ways, I doubt Mother Mary will ever find a home for you." Moose really was being extra mean, and Reggie almost felt sorry for the other kids in the home that he and Prudence were going too.

"You've got a big mouth, Moose, we will be glad to see the back of you," Reggie told him.

"Hear, hear," Seamus concurred. "Our gain is their loss, Higginbottom," and the four friends laughed, as they always did at the sound of his surname.

It really was not a laughing matter though, and they knew it. Moose was right. The likelihood of them being kept together was very slim and it distressed them greatly.

From that moment on D-vision spent every waking moment together. Reggie and Seamus wanted to be there for the girls emotionally and all four of them promised that wherever they ended up, they would keep in touch and try to arrange to see each other as often as they could. They knew that keeping promises like that were never easy, especially if they moved a long way away, but they vowed to do their best.

As the end of August drew near, Mary was no closer to sorting homes for Reggie, Seamus, Paxton and Jasmin and she was beginning to despair as to what she would do. The other six children were gradually getting used to the idea of leaving. Some were even starting to get a little excited to meet their new families, although they would never have admitted it to Mary.

No timeline had been laid out by the bank, so no one really knew how much time they had left together, but all too quickly Mary began to receive telephone calls to say the placements for the six children were ready. Everyone concerned believed that a rapid change over was vital and suddenly it was arranged that they would all leave, except for D-vision, on the first weekend in September.

The children packed up their belongings with the help of Sister Alice. As they had all come to Hawthorns with nothing, everything they were taking had been bought for them by Mary, and everyone was shocked at how bare their rooms looked when they were finished.

It turned out to be the most painful and poignant weekend of their lives. Mary tried the best she could to be strong, as gradually one by one, each child left to go to their new homes. Everyone shed hundreds of tears as they said their goodbyes, knowing it was the end of an era for all of them. Life would be very different in the future.

The last two to leave were Moose and Prudence, and even they behaved themselves, mostly. Moose had shaken Reggie's hand and told him that he hoped he would soon find a home although he doubted it as he was so weird. Reggie had just laughed almost expecting him to say something cruel, but they had been through so much it really didn't matter anymore. They had hugged Mother Mary and Sister Alice and thanked them for everything, and then they were gone, leaving Mary, Alice, Reggie, Seamus, Paxton and Jasmin who stood holding each other, scared of what the future had in store for them.

The house felt very empty that night and the six of them sat in the lounge together eating pizza. None of them knew how much longer they would be together, so they wanted to spend every second possible in each other's company. The house was eerily quiet, but D-vision had to admit they did sort of like it. There were no younger children crying and needing attention, and with the absence of Moose and Prudence they were all much calmer.

"Be quite nice if it could stay like this forever, wouldn't it?" Paxton commented after Mother Mary and Sister Alice left the room.

"Sure would," Seamus replied. "I have never known it this quiet. It's a pleasure for my supersonic hearing," he said, and they all giggled.

"Seriously though, Reggie, what do you think will happen to us?" Jasmin relied heavily on Reggie and being the youngest was still frantic at the prospect of leaving.

"I really don't know, Jas," he told her. "Maybe fate will throw us a kind hand. But one way or another I'm sure we will find out very soon. Just keep your fingers crossed for something good."

"I will, Reggie, I promise," she said giving him a tight hug.

Very early the following morning Mary noticed a letter resting on the door mat in the hall. Picking it up, she knew it was too early to have been delivered by the postman. The envelope was handwritten, but there was no other mark to identify who or where it was from. She strolled into her study before anyone else in the house had risen and opened it carefully.

Dear Miss Bridges,

Please accept my humble apologies for contacting you in such a direct way and please do me the great honour of continuing to read the entirety of what I have to say. Please do not dismiss my words as a joke or believe that I am some sort of lunatic. I am honest, sincere, and most definitely serious.

I am a customer of the Bank of Brighton and learnt of your plight at Hawthorns, the home you run for orphaned children. I will start by saying that I admire what you have done for those children, and wish I had the courage to be as brave as you have been taking them on. I am the owner of a large international corporation that I inherited from my adopted father and have been very privileged in my life, but I did not have the easiest of beginnings. I left my childhood home at the age of sixteen, for reasons of which I will not enter into at this stage but found myself homeless and parentless. I was fortunate enough to be taken in by the man that I came to know and love as my father, so I am perfectly placed to understand what you have been through and what you mean to the children you have taken in.

Therefore, I write to you today to offer a small amount of assistance by way of extending an invitation to your four remaining children to join me on an all-expenses paid trip to Thailand and Australia. Of course, I will be delighted to extend the invitation to you also and believe that it will be an enlightening trip at this difficult time in all your lives.

We are due to leave in seven days from now; you will be collected by my own limousine and escorted to a private airfield near Gatwick. My private jet will then fly you to Suvarnabhami Airport in Bangkok, where I will meet you and drive you to your own private suite at the Siam Kempinski Hotel.

You will stay in Thailand for six days and then fly onto Sydney for the duration of the fourteen-day trip. I offer apologies for not being able to accompany you and the children for the whole journey, but my hectic business schedule will not afford me the time to fly to England.

I can imagine at this stage what you must be thinking and assure you that this is a truly genuine offer made with the utmost seriousness and integrity. Of course, you will be sceptical believing such an arrangement from a complete stranger. Therefore, I have made provision for my personal aid, Mr Sai Baba to visit you tomorrow at 10.00am sharp, to go over the rest of the itinerary and assure you of my best intentions.

I trust you will be able to accommodate him, and most heartedly hope that you will, for the sake of the children, accept my offer.

With my utmost sincerity,
Mr Amir Mohan

Mary perched herself on the side of her desk to steady her legs and gather her thoughts. What an odd letter. Beautifully written, but odd all the same. Of course, they could not go. What on earth was this man thinking? How could she possibly let the children go galivanting to the other side of the world with a stranger she had never even met? No, they definitely could not go. But could they?

She read the letter again, from start to finish and something about Mr Mohan's words made her want to trust him. It certainly would be the opportunity of a lifetime, and after all she had put the children through in the last few weeks, they really did deserve it. So, she promised herself that she would have a long hard think about it.

And think about it she did. For the rest of the day, she thought about nothing else. She did not say anything to anyone about the letter and decided to wait until Mr Baba arrived the next morning, knowing she would have a multitude of questions to ask before she made her final decision.

Mary knew that when Mr Baba arrived, and the children got wind of what was happening she would be pestered into allowing them to go and wanted to have her arguments to prevent them ready. She hid herself away for the whole afternoon and did as much research as possible. She telephoned the Bank of Brighton, who happily confirmed that Mr Mohan was one of their best and most influential customers. She checked the financial pages of the newspaper to learn that his company was a multi-million-dollar organisation, and that he had been honoured with The Queen's Award for Business and both Business Culture and Fortune Global awards. He had also graced the front pages of GQ magazine, and unfortunately, for Mary, she could not find one negative about him.

When the doorbell rang at exactly ten o'clock the following morning, she was ready for Mr Baba. She showed him into her study and offered him coffee. He had declined graciously and said that he wanted to get straight to business. Mary liked him instantly but was still prepared to grill him about Mr Mohan and the trip. They talked, animatedly for over an hour, and Mary found they went around and around in circles. Mr Baba had a solid and convincing answer for all her questions, and she was finding it very difficult to put him off.

"How about my meeting the children concerned and discussing the trip with them?" Mr Mohan's aid said at last, feeling he was not getting anywhere either.

"Yes, I think that would be a good idea. We seem to be going over and over this, and it does concern them too. Please excuse me for a moment and I will ask Sister Alice to bring them in," Mary said politely, and left the room.

They all appeared in the room in front of the stranger a few moments later.

"Is this man going to take us to a new home?" Jasmin asked with terror in her eyes. It was just what they were all thinking but she had been the only one brave enough to ask.

"No, Jasmin, he is not. He is here on a totally different matter." Mary decided to simply come right out and tell them what was going on. "This gentleman works for a businessman called Amir Mohan. It seems that the four of you have come to his attention and before you leave here for new homes, he wishes to offer to take you on a holiday to Thailand and Australia."

"Oh my God! Really?" Reggie shouted.

"I know I have good hearing, but did I hear that right?" Seamus asked.

"When? When do we leave?" Paxton wanted to know excitedly.

"Calm down, guys. I have not said yes yet. We do not know this man and we still have a lot to discuss. I think we have to talk about this some more," Mary told them all.

"I think it will be good for the children," Sister Alice wanted to show them her support.

"Oh yes, Mother Mary, it will be a wonderful opportunity," Reggie chipped in.

"Please, please, please can we. Go on, say yes," Paxton and Jasmin chimed in unison.

"All right! Enough! You can go," Mary blurted out not able to take their badgering any longer.

In fact, she had pretty much made her decision the night before. She had given the idea a lot of thought and knew that she had no right to stop them. It would be the holiday of a lifetime and would almost certainly be the last time they would spend any quality time together. She had to let them go. She had just wanted to wait and meet Amir's aid before she gave them the good news. She was satisfied that the whole situation was a safe and honest one and seemed to have complete trust in Mr Baba.

"Thank you, Mother Mary," Reggie said for all of them.

"When do we leave, and are you coming with us?" Jasmin asked.

"You will leave in six days, by private jet, courtesy of Mr Mohan, but I'm afraid I cannot come with you. I must stay here to make arrangements with the bank to put the house on the market. I must continue to look for homes for the four of you, and I have Susan's funeral to prepare for. Don't worry though, I'm sure Mr Baba here will take wonderful care of you," she told them. "Now run along and leave Mr Baba and I to make the final arrangements."

"See, Reggie, I promised you I would keep my fingers crossed for something good," Jasmin whispered as they left the room.

CHAPTER FOUR
A MAGICAL JOURNEY

The next six days were a hive of activity at Hawthorns. Sister Alice helped Seamus and Jasmin do their packing and told Reggie and Paxton what she thought they should take. Sai Baba came to visit twice more, to get to know the children. He took them to the park, the cinema and out for pasta. They all liked him very much and looked forward to spending more time with him on their holiday.

Mary had spoken to Amir Mohan on the telephone several times, and he apologised time and time again for being unable to leave his current business meetings in Dubai. He was also sorry that she would not be joining them. Each time she spoke to him she liked him a little more and began to wish she could go too. Amir assured her that his aid would look after the children on the flight and that he would be waiting for them at Bangkok Airport. And by the time the day of their departure arrived, both Mary and Alice were confident the children would be well taken care of.

Mary had offered Alice to take the trip in her place, but she had gratefully declined. She had never much taken to flying. She thought it was something that only birds should do, and besides, she wanted to be on hand to help Mary with whatever she needed in the difficult weeks ahead.

On the day of the children's departure, they were so excited they didn't stop talking. They rose early and checked their baggage to make sure they had not forgotten anything and trying to get them to eat breakfast had proved impossible. Mary talked to them all, telling them to be careful and look after each other, and made them promise to call her the moment they checked into the hotel in Thailand.

At exactly one o'clock in the afternoon, Sai Baba rang the doorbell and was greeted by four of the most jubilant children he had ever seen. He had never married or had children himself, so this mission was one that he was looking forward to immensely. He had worked for Amir for nearly ten years, always ready to carry out his every command, and found him a thoughtful and generous employer. But of all he had ever done for Mr Mohan, this job was going to be one of the most fun.

"Wow, look at that car!" Reggie shouted as he looked at the limousine waiting by the kerb.

"What is it like, Reggie? Is it nice?" Seamus wanted to know.

"Oh, Seamus it is the best-looking car I have ever seen. It is gleaming white and as long as a bus."

"Wait until you get inside," Sai added. "That is when the fun really starts. First though you must all say your farewells to Mary and Alice while I have the driver put your cases in the boot."

"A driver, just for us," Paxton laughed. "I feel like a queen. Come on, let's get this show on the road."

One by one they hugged Mary and Sister Alice and assured them that they would be fine. They did not want them to be worrying the whole time they were away as they had important jobs to attend to. Both Jasmin and Paxton were crying. It was heart wrenching leaving Mother Mary. The girls loved and relied on her so much, it made Mary worry as to how hard it would be when the time came for them to leave for good. Determined not to cry for fear of upsetting the girls further, Mary tried to stay strong. She held their hands as she walked them to the car.

Sai, as they now called him, assured Mary one last time that there was no cause to fret and that they would all return safely in two weeks. And then they were gone, leaving Mary and Alice alone to a childless house for the first time in Mary's life.

Back inside the house Mary was already worried. Sai Baba could give all the assurance in the world, but they were her children, and they were going away, travelling to the far side of the planet. Of course, she was going to worry; how could she not?

In the limousine the children were in their element. The onboard bar had been stocked with Coca-Cola, lemonade and fresh fruit juice, and there was a wicker picnic hamper full of more edible goodies than they could have imagined. It was a wonderful start to this magical journey, and they couldn't wait for it to continue.

The car journey to the airport took just over an hour and by the time they arrived at the private airfield the children had filled up on fizzy drinks and treats. Sai hoped that they had not over-indulged so much that the flight might make them sick. And as the limousine stopped right next to the airstairs, the happy passengers only had to take a few steps to board the plane.

When they left the comfort of the car, a large aeroplane waited in front of them with the name Mohan Industries painted on the side in large blue letters. It was a wonderful sight, and the children could not wait to climb aboard.

Inside was a spacious cabin containing ten, cream leather armchairs; each with its own pull-out table. There was a long galley that housed a bar and containers to store on-board food, and a state-of-the-art entertainment system with more movies to watch than the children knew existed. Sai even told them that there was a small sleeping compartment at the back of the plane. That, however, did not interest any of them. They had no intention of sleeping for one second.

They chose their seats and made themselves comfortable and before long the door closed. Each of them felt their hearts pound as the engines roared into life.

"Good morning, Reggie, Seamus, Paxton and Jasmin, and welcome aboard this Gulfstream II Cabin Jet. I am your captain, John Stokes, and we will be travelling today at a maximum speed of five hundred and eighty miles per hour. The weather is mild, with very light winds and we have an overall flight time to Bangkok of twelve and a half hours. We will make a brief stop in New Delhi to refuel and then immediately continue on our way. So, sit back, relax, enjoy the ride and remember that Sai and I are here should you need anything."

The moment Captain Stokes had stopped speaking, the Gulfstream private jet began to taxi towards the runway that the children could see from the windows. The plane took a left turn, the engines boomed even louder, it gathered great speed very quickly and within seconds everyone could feel the wheels had left the runway.

Poor Seamus needed to put his fingers in his ears for the rumble had been deafening to him and Reggie had to tell him it was all right to remove them as the engine noise decreased and their altitude grew.

"Everyone okay?" Sai asked looking around the cabin. "I have a quick talk to give you about flight safety while we are on board and then, you can unbuckle your seat belts and move around. Seamus, I have a sheet here for you with the safety instructions in braille that you might like to go over as well as hearing what I have to say."

Mr Mohan had cleverly thought of everything and all four sat quietly and listened to what Sai had to say. They sincerely doubted they would need to know the procedure but felt they should do him the courtesy of paying attention.

"Can we watch a movie, please?" Jasmin asked when Sai had finished.

"Yes, of course, you can choose whatever you like," he told them, and handed Reggie a large remote control and quickly showed him how the entertainment system worked. It turned out there would be enough time on board for them all to have a film of their choice, so Jasmin chose first.

The children sat at the bar for a while and pretended to be very grown up, as Sai made them all fruit cocktails - and that was followed by an early supper of hamburgers and French fries. Each one of them felt very privileged and if it was any indication of how the rest of the holiday was going to be, they knew they were in for an amazing time.

The hours on board passed quickly and with so much to occupy themselves, they didn't have a moment to get bored. Jasmin had fallen asleep once her movie finished, which pleased Reggie and Seamus as they had picked a film that was quite violent and contained a lot of bad language. It was not the sort of film that Mary would have let them watch at Hawthorns, so they decided to make the most of it.

"It's such a shame that neither Mother Mary nor Sister Alice could come with us," Paxton whispered to the boys, not wanting to wake Jasmin. "I'm really going to miss them."

"I know," Reggie replied, "I will miss them too, but at least we get to watch better movies," he said, and they all giggled knowing the ladies would not have approved.

"You guys had better keep that quiet when you get home," Sai told them, "or you will get me into big trouble. Especially with Sister Alice. She rather scares me," he said jokingly.

"Sure, mum's the word," Paxton said, and began to flick through a fashion magazine she had found.

It really was the most wonderful way to travel, and the children knew how lucky they were to be having such an adventure. They appreciated the opportunity so much and amused themselves until their arrival in Bangkok when they would meet their generous benefactor, Amir Mohan.

After several hours of silence from the cockpit, John Stokes interrupted them once again to inform them they were approaching New Delhi and would be making the stop to refuel half an hour later. It would be a quick and easy stop over, without the need for anyone to leave the plane. Nevertheless, a very necessary one, as the Gulfstream II could only fly non-stop for a maximum of nine hours.

A while after making the announcement, and preparing to bring the plane into land, Captain Stokes noticed that he had somehow moved off his flight path. He tried to adjust the necessary equipment, and as he did, he realised the plane was heading due Northeast and he did not know why. He was not able to make a drop in altitude and very quickly knew that something was wrong. Looking at his radar, he was shocked to see that the position of the plane had completely disappeared from the screen.

"Ground control, this is flight GS DV4 on route to New Delhi. I seem to have lost visuals. Please advise?" he said into his mouthpiece.

John Stokes had been a commercial and now private pilot for over twenty years. He was an experienced and fearless devotee of aviation and had encountered many strange phenomena in his years travelling around the world, but when he received no response from ground control, he began to fear the worst. He tried to remain calm, as he knew he had to be in any emergency situation, and not raise the alarm yet. But was this actually an emergency? The plane was not going down; it was just off course. He tried everything in the book to rectify the problem, to no avail. By now the plane was badly adrift and John had totally lost control of it. It was as if a strange force had taken over and was pulling the plane away from its destination. And what worried John the most was that he knew they were heading towards the Himalayan Mountains. It was the highest and largest terrain of mountains in the world, with very few safe places for a plane to land, and before long they would be out of fuel. John knew now that it was definitely an emergency.

"Mr Baba, could I please see you in the cockpit for a moment?" came the announcement over the intercom.

"We should be landing in Delhi shortly, kids. Stay in your seats and I will just pop and see what the pilot wants," Sai told the four D-vision members.

Once inside the pilot's cabin at the front of the plane, Sai could immediately see from the look on John Stokes face that something was wrong.

"Everything all right, John?"

"Well actually, no. I have never come across anything like this in my career. I seem to have lost control of the plane. We have gone off radar and I have lost all communication with ground control," John told him as calmly as he could.

"What do you mean you have lost control, we are still in the air, aren't we?" Sai questioned, not really understanding what was happening.

"Yes, we are still in the air, and we have not lost altitude, but the plane is being pulled off course. We are headed for the Himalayas, and we are running low on fuel."

"I don't understand, John. What are you saying?" Sai was getting worried.

"I'm saying I have no control over where this plane is flying or how to stop it. And when we run out of fuel, then God knows, Sai. We could be in real trouble here," John told him bluntly.

"Are we going to crash, John?" Sai Baba was suddenly terrified for the children.

"Well, I can find no fault with the engines, but yes, we cannot stay in the air indefinitely. If I regain control, I will try to find a suitable place to land, but if that does not happen, I'm afraid we will be going down."

"Oh my God, the children! What will I tell the children?" Sai felt sick to the stomach with panic.

"Just stay calm, Sai," the pilot could sense his fear. "Don't tell them the worst-case scenario. Just look after them and I will do all I can."

Sai Baba tried to brush the look of despair from his face as he re-entered the main cabin. His boss had offered these wonderful children the holiday of a lifetime, and he had been given the responsibility of looking after them … and quite possibly disaster was about to strike. All he had to do was get them safely to Bangkok and there was a great chance now that none of them would make it.

"Okay, guys," he said putting on a brave face. "I need you all to stay in your seats for a while and fasten your safety belts. It seems we have gone off course a little, and have missed New Delhi, so we will have to stay in the air until we can land at the next available airport."

"Will we have enough fuel for that?" Reggie understood very well how long they had been flying.

"Oh yes, it will not be far from here. The only small problem we have is that we are flying over the Himalayan Mountains, so we need to stay very high which will take a little longer, and it may get a little bumpy so best to stay seated."

Sai continued to try and entertain the children and had trouble keeping Paxton in her seat to prevent her looking out the window at the mountains below. While in the cockpit John Stokes mustered every piece of aviation knowledge he had to try and rectify the situation. Looking at the fuel gauge he knew that things were getting desperate, and he still had no control or contact from the ground. The plane seemed to be drifting further and further over the vast mountain range and there was nothing he could do to stop it.

Almost an hour had passed since John realised that they had a problem, when suddenly the fuel indicator began to flash. There was a huge drop in altitude which caused the plane to plummet several hundred feet and Sai and the children let out gasps of shock.

"What was that?" Paxton looked terrified and Jasmin started to cry.

"It's okay, the pilot knows what he is doing. He is probably just bringing us down quicker than we would have liked." Sai himself was not convinced.

From there on in, it was a pretty turbulent ride. The plane listed to the side a couple of times, and things in the cabin fell to the floor. Several more times the plane went through great drops in altitude, and by now everyone was panicked, believing something bad was happening.

Paxton had joined Jasmin crying by then, and Sai did his best to comfort them from where he sat.

"Sai, the girls are really scared, actually we all are. Will you please go and ask John what is going on?" Reggie pleaded with their temporary guardian.

"Sure, don't leave your seats, any of you. And don't worry." Suddenly Sai's reassurance seemed like a waste of breath.

He unbuckled his seat belt and stood from the safety of his chair, placing his hand against the side wall to steady himself. When he entered the cockpit once again, he saw John Stokes shaking his head and knew they were doomed.

"Come on, John, there must be something you can do? You can fly anything," Sai almost pleaded.

"I'm sorry, Sai, the plane is virtually out of fuel, we are dropping fast. I have no way of stopping it," the sorrowful pilot told his friend. "I have no idea what has happened. It is as if a strange force has taken over the plane and stripped all the control away from me. I am powerless, I'm afraid. We are deep in the mountain range now and coming down quickly. Our only hope is that whatever has taken hold of us, finds somewhere flat to put us down, but I can't see that happening. At a guess we are only a few hundred feet up now at most. I'm sorry, Sai, I suggest you tell the children to prepare for the worst."

"Thanks, my friend," Sai said tapping John on the shoulder. "I'm sorry that our magical journey has turned into a nightmare," he said as he left the cockpit to return to the children. Unfortunately, before he reached them, there was an almighty crash. All four children would have been thrown from their seats had they not been strapped in. Reggie banged his head against the side wall. Seamus found himself flung forward causing the belt to crush against his stomach and make him yelp. Paxton dropped the cup of hot chocolate she had been holding and burnt her leg, and then came Jasmin's scream. A body flew past her shoulder at great speed and crashed into the bar where it fell lifeless to the floor.

"What was that?" Seamus shouted not able to identify the strange noise.

"I think it was Sai, he fell to the back of the plane," Reggie told him.

"My God, is he okay? Can we check on him?" he said feeling to undo his seat belt.

"No!" Reggie shouted. "The plane is still moving. I don't know what has happened, but we must stay in our seats to protect ourselves."

None of them knew what had happened yet could feel they were no longer in the air. The plane was definitely still moving, however, so they guessed they were now sliding, very quickly along the ground.

They did not have long to wait to find out what would happen next, for within a few moments a second loud bang occurred. The plane jolted so hard all four children were dazed and shaken, and when they had composed themselves, they realised the plane had finally stopped.

Reggie told Seamus to look after the girls, while he left his seat to move to the back of the plane to help Sai. His unconscious body lay motionless, and he had a large gash on the side of his head with blood pouring onto the floor. Reggie called his name, shaking his shoulder, but could not wake him.

"Is he dead?" Jasmin screamed. "He looks dead. Oh no, he is dead, isn't he?" She began to cry and shake again.

"I don't know, Jas," Reggie told her. "I'm really not sure. He is bleeding pretty badly though. Can you try and find something to wrap around his head to stem the blood loss? Pax can you go to the cockpit and see how Captain Stokes is?" Reggie automatically took charge. Being the eldest of the D-vision club he knew that by giving them jobs to concentrate on it would stop them thinking about what had happened. "Seamus, if you turn right out of your seat, walk about five paces straight ahead and then turn to your right again. You should find the door. There is a large bar to push down to open it. We can then get a look at where we are."

The three younger children did as they were asked while Reggie tried again to rouse Sai. Seamus found and opened the door to the outside and within seconds a gust of freezing air entered the cabin. A second later a loud scream rang out from the cockpit. Reggie and Jasmin rushed to the entrance to see the motionless body of their pilot. He had clearly been thrown from his chair as the plane suffered the second blow. There was smashed glass from the windscreen all over the floor, and John Stokes was covered in blood. They could only assume he was dead as they stood looking at the solid wall of white snow that covered the front of the plane.

The three of them moved from the cockpit back to Seamus at the open door and looked out. "What is it?" asked Seamus. "Where are we?"

"Well, at a guess, we are deep in the Himalayas as Sai said earlier that we might be. There is nothing to see but mountains and snow. It looks like we may have come down in some sort of ravine, between the mountains and hurtled along the ground until we crashed into that snow-covered rock face in front of us."

"God, it's freezing out there. What on earth are we going to do, Reggie?" Paxton didn't like their chances if they went outside.

"Well, it's getting pretty cold in here too. We should pull the door closed and have a look around for some blankets or something to use to keep warm," Reggie answered confidently. "Girls, can you do that, please, and I will get back to Sai?"

The girls disappeared to the back of the plane beyond the bar, where none of them had ventured before. They assumed they would find the sleeping cabin Sai had mentioned and hoped to find something they could use for warmth. Reggie wrapped the towel around Sai's head that Jasmin had dropped by his body when she ran to the cockpit. Thankfully the blood stopped pumping out, but Sai Baba was still unconscious.

"Found anything?" Reggie shouted in the direction of the back of the plane.

"Yes, we're in luck." Paxton and Jasmin appeared with their arms full. "We have found these padded coats that look really warm and several pairs of snow boots," Paxton said as the two girls dropped everything they had found on the floor. "How is Sai, Reggie? Is he going to be okay?"

"No joy, I'm afraid. I've wrapped up his head to stem the bleeding, but I still can't wake him."

"He's dead, isn't he? Poor Sai." Jasmin was devastated.

"No, Jas, I'm sure he is still alive, although I don't know how long for if help doesn't come soon." Reggie was not only worried about Sai but also about himself and three best friends. The day had begun on such a high and now they found themselves in the most perilous of situations. The only thing he could be thankful for was that the four of them were still alive.

"Guys, I don't want to worry you. I can hear a strange sizzling noise," Seamus cut into Reggie's thoughts.

"What is it, Seamus?"

They all listened but couldn't hear anything.

"It is quite faint, but it sounds like the noise a bonfire makes when the logs are crackling."

All four of them knew very well to trust Seamus. When he said he could hear something, he always could. It was the description he used that worried Reggie most.

"Are you sure, Seamus?" Reggie watched as his friend nodded his head. "Right, all of you stay here. I'm going outside to have a quick look around."

"Be careful," Jasmin shouted as Reggie jumped from the door.

The wait seemed like an eternity. In reality, Reggie returned less than a minute later.

"Not good news I'm afraid, guys … there is smoke coming from one of the engines. I can't see any flames, but we must get out quickly. It could go up at any moment. Pax, you and Jas grab the coats and boots and I will help Seamus. Come on, we must go now."

"What about Sai?" Jasmin said looking down at his still body while Paxton gathered up the coats.

"I'm sorry, Jas, we can't help him now. We must think of our own safety. Come on, we must leave," Reggie told them as he took Seamus's arm.

The magical journey had ended abruptly, and the four friends took one last look at the body of Sai Baba as they jumped from the plane.

CHAPTER FIVE
THE WHITE WILDERNESS

Reggie, Seamus, Paxton and Jasmin ran from the plane for a minute or two, until Reggie's grip on Seamus's arm released and Seamus tripped and fell. Reggie helped him up and prepared to continue to walk when Jasmin stopped too and refused to carry on, shaking her head.

"Please, Reggie can we stop for a second? I'm out of breath."

"Sure. Sorry, Jas. I think we are far enough away now," he said as they turned to see flames now bellowing from the engine just above the wing.

"Well done, Reggie." Paxton was relieved. "We left just in time. Good job, Seamus, thanks. I am so glad we can always count on your hearing."

"Yeah, good job," Reggie said, helping Seamus brush the snow from his clothes. "Now, put on a coat and a pair of boots each and we will have a look around and make a plan."

Reggie, Paxton and Jasmin spent a few moments looking around and took in their surroundings. As far as their eyes could see it was a terrain of mountains, covered in the purest white snow.

"Anything of interest?" Seamus asked.

"No, not really. Just mountains, snow and more snow," Jasmin told him.

"It is so beautiful, Seamus, I wish you could see it," Paxton said thoughtfully. "We are definitely in the Himalayas. It looks just like the pictures in the book Sister Alice gave me."

"That's nice, Pax, but we have to come up with a plan," Reggie cut in.

"I think we should stay here and wait for help to arrive. They will know we are missing before too long and send help. And besides, we can't leave Sai. We should stay nearby, and wait for a rescue party to reach us," Paxton said confidently.

"I think we need to go and try to find help in a village or something," Reggie replied.

"No! We are safer here, and we can't leave Sai. And besides the Himalayas are so vast we could walk for days and never find help."

As Paxton spoke the words an explosive bang escaped from the plane sending plumes of smoke high into the air.

"Guys, please don't argue," Seamus wanted everyone to calm down. "I'm with Reggie. I think the three of you should go and find help."

"What do you mean three of us?" Jasmin questioned not sure what Seamus meant.

"The three of you should go and find help. You have to leave me here. It will be too difficult for me, and I will just slow you down too much. I'll wait by the plane in case Sai makes it out when he wakes up."

"No!" shouted Paxton and Jasmin.

"What are you thinking, Seamus?" Reggie scolded. "There is no way. We are not leaving anyone behind. There is a reason the four of us made it out of that plane crash and we are going to stick together and find out what it is. What would Mother Mary and Sister Alice say if we split up? Remember what Mary said as we left, 'Stay together and look after each other.' We have a commitment to do that and make it back together. We are D-vision, and we can do anything. Four of us left Brighton yesterday and four of us are going to return. Agreed?"

"You bet, Reggie. To D-vision!" they shouted in unison.

^∧^

Meanwhile, back in Brighton, Mary was sitting in her study waiting for the phone to ring. She knew that the flight would take approximately twelve and a half hours, which meant they landed around two thirty in the morning UK time. She had felt uneasy from the instant the limousine left the house, unable to sleep for a second, pacing anxiously around the room. She added the six hours Thailand was ahead of England, making it around nine o'clock in the morning when they landed in Bangkok, and hoped the telephone would ring at any second.

"Are you going to go to bed?" Sister Alice asked, popping her head in the door.

"Oh no, Alice, I couldn't sleep if I wanted to. Not until I hear from the children or Sai."

"Well, they will realise that it is the early hours of the morning here, so they may not want to wake you. Maybe they will check in first, have a rest and then call. Can I get you a cup of coffee or something?" Alice knew she had to look after her.

"No, thank you, I'm fine. They know I will not settle until I hear from them, but you are probably right. They must be very tired from the journey. Why don't you run along and get some sleep and I will wake you when I hear from them? There is no point us both being tired with so much to do here."

"Sure, I think I will, but please wake me when they call," Sister Alice was as eager as Mary to know they had arrived safely.

"I will, I promise," Mary told her. "Sleep well."

The darkness of night came and went, and with every hour that passed Mary became more distressed. She tried Sai's company mobile phone several times – which was a new concept to her, and she was thankful that he had one. Unfortunately, though, it went straight through to his voicemail. She then tried the hotel in Bangkok and got disconnected.

At eight the next morning the study door opened again. "Thanks for letting me sleep. How are they all?" Alice asked her weary looking friend.

"Oh Alice, I wish I knew. I haven't heard from them yet. It's two o'clock in the afternoon there. They must be up and about by now. I'm beginning to get really worried," Mary said as she flopped down onto the sofa.

"What about that mobile phone thing that Sai has, or the hotel?" Alice was worried too but needed to stay positive.

"Tried both, and no luck."

Then, suddenly Mary remembered the vision she'd had when she visited Susan earlier in the year.

"Are you all right, Mary?" Alice could see she had turned a deathly pale colour.

"I just had the most terrible feeling come over me, Alice. Do you remember when I visited my friend Susan back in June, I had that premonition of a plane coming down while I was driving home? Oh my God, what if that was an early warning? What if that was the children's plane?"

"No, no, no! Do not even think that. That was a long time ago and you said so yourself that you rarely had visions these days. I'm sure it was just a coincidence as you were driving near the airport. You must not think like that. The good Lord will take care of our children, I'm sure of it."

Mary felt a little silly for letting her imagination run away with her and was glad Alice was there to make her get a hold of herself.

"Yes, Alice, I'm sorry. Of course, you are right. Let's go and make some breakfast to take our mind off things and then I will try and call Sai again."

Neither of the women ate as they sat in silence at the kitchen table, unable to find any words to say to each other. The rest of the day dragged by with Mary trying everything she could to contact Sai and the children. She called the private airfield. She called Gatwick Airport. She called Mohan Industries. She called the hotel in Bangkok. She even called the police. The response was the same every time. There were no answers. By the time night fell Mary could not remove her vision from her mind and the sense of foreboding she felt became all consuming. Alice said a prayer, and both women sat glued to the news channels expecting to see a report of a plane crash somewhere between England and Thailand.

Finally, having both dozed off on the sofas, unable to stay awake a moment later, a loud knock on the front door woke them. The sun was up, and Mary looked at her watch to see it was seven in the morning.

"Who on earth can that be at this hour?" she said making her way into the hall with Alice close behind her.

Rubbing her eyes, she opened the door to be greeted by a tall, handsome stranger with olive skin and black hair. "May I help you?" she asked.

"Please forgive the earliness of the hour. I have been travelling all night from Dubai. My name is Amir Mohan. Please may I come in?"

Mary and Alice escorted their visitor to the study, where they stood in silence and listened to what he had to say. The details he gave seemed to be very vague, and no matter how many times he apologised, all Mary could take in was that the plane was uncontactable, and the children were missing. Mary collapsed into the stranger's arms, and he gently placed her down on the sofa while Alice left the room to make them all some very sweet tea.

A lifetime elapsed in the next few minutes and when Mary had finished her tea, she looked into Mr Mohan's eyes with such despair his heart went out to her. It was hard for him too. His aid and best friend, Sai, was missing, but worst of all he had brought this upset upon them by offering the holiday in the first place. He wanted to tell Mary that everything would be all right; that the children would be found safe and well. While all he could say was that he would do everything in his power, using every resource available, to find the children and bring them home.

He left a short time later, having informed them that he was flying immediately to India to try and locate the last place the authorities had contact with the plane and begin an investigation from there. Mary and Alice sat speechless in the office when he left, and Mary realised she felt sorry for him. He seemed like a kind and genuine man, and under different circumstances she would have liked to get to know him better. Sadly though, for now, every ounce of her attention would be given to praying with Sister Alice for the children's safe return.

∧∧∧

"Right, now that is settled, which way shall we head?" Jasmin asked looking around in all directions.

"Your guess is as good as mine, Jas. Reckon it will be potluck. You choose," Reggie told the youngest member of their group, not wanting them to think that he made all the decisions.

"Wait! I think I saw something," Paxton interrupted them. "No, it couldn't be…"

"What, Pax? What did you see?" Seamus was curious. "It's funny, I thought I heard something like the sound of snow crunching in the distance," he added.

"I thought I saw the shadowy figure of a child, or a small person run behind the rocks at the end of ravine. It was a fair way off, so I was probably mistaken."

"No, the sound I heard could definitely have been footsteps on the snow. You may be right, Pax. Come on, we must investigate. Lead the way, Reg." Seamus was confident he had heard something too and believed that Paxton had seen something. Although he could not imagine what anyone would be doing outside, if it were as remote as his friends said it was.

"All right, guys, I think you are both mad," Reggie declared. "But we are a team so let's go. You saw it, Pax, lead the way. Seamus take my arm," he said reaching out, making contact with his best friend.

Guiding Seamus with care, the four friends slowly walked the length of the ravine, away from the plane. It was a clear day, with the sun high in the sky. Its glare on the snow bothered Paxton and Jasmin, forcing them to shield their eyes much of the time. There was also a freezing bite to the wind, making them extremely thankful for the warm coats they had found.

As they walked, each of them took turns to call out to the stranger that Paxton had seen. Getting no response, when they reached the end of the gully, they found the mountains around them started to close in and they all felt a little claustrophobic.

"Which way, Pax? Can you remember?" Reggie asked.

"Yes, just around the end of that rock face," Paxton pointed to where she saw the figure disappear.

"Look! Footprints," Jasmin pointed. "They are small and barely visible, but definitely footprints.

"Well spotted, Jas. Come on, let's follow them." Reggie seemed pleased that Paxton had been right. It was the first sign of any good news they'd had since the crash and finally believed they were a step closer to finding help.

The four of them followed the footprints until they suddenly vanished. "I don't believe it. How can they just stop?" Jasmin was confused and disappointed.

"Look up there, on that ledge. I saw it, the figure again. Come on, guys, let's climb the ledge and follow them," Paxton shouted, pointing to a rocky ridge above.

It was no easy feat to climb up, and it surprised them how agile Seamus was. With a bit of teamwork, it didn't prove too much of a problem at all. They walked cautiously along the narrow sill, calling out all the time. Still, they got no answer from the person they were in pursuit of.

Once at the end of the ledge the children climbed down and noticed another figure run across an open expanse that meandered between the mountains. Continuing in the same direction, still wondering why these strange figures made no attempt to stop and offer help, they began to feel tired, hungry and disheartened. It had been tough walking on the icy terrain, and with no idea of how long they had been following the amazing disappearing people, they suddenly wondered if they would ever catch up with them.

"Can we stop for a while? My legs ache," Jasmin whined.

"Yes, can we, Reg? I'm tired too," Paxton added flopping down into the snow.

"Sure, let's sit for a while, but not too long," Reggie told the girls. "We must have been walking for a few hours, but we have to consider the weather. It can close in on us at any moment and if it begins to snow, we could be done for. So, we should continue as soon as we can."

"Do you think whoever we saw was the same person each time or several different people?" Paxton seemed curious about the strangers they had been following.

"Yeah, and I wonder why they didn't stop when we called them," Seamus added.

"We are halfway across the world, Seamus. They probably don't speak a word of English." It was the only explanation that Reggie could come up with.

"Of course," Seamus replied shivering violently. "Never thought of that."

"Are you getting cold, Seamus?" Reggie was worried about how his friend was coping with the tough terrain.

"Just a little, but don't worry about me."

"I do worry. We must be on the move again shortly. We will lose too much body heat if we sit still for long," Reggie told them all.

"Oh my, look, I've spotted another one up there on that rock. It's very high, but I'm sure I'm right," Paxton declared, hoping she was not going mad from the cold or sun blindness.

"All right, it is high … I will give it a go. You three sit here for a bit longer and I will climb up and look around from the top," Reggie told them taking charge again. "And if you get really cold huddle together to keep each other warm. Be back as quickly as I can."

Reggie left Seamus, Paxton and Jasmin sitting on the ground and began the climb up the huge rock that stood immediately behind them. He had to use all his skills of strength and balance to make the ascent. It was tough going and he was soon out of breath. He lost his footing a couple of times on the slippery ice and was glad of the ridged soles on his boots. The main problem was his hands throbbing and turning bright red where he used them to steady himself.

He had no idea how long it took to reach the top and wondered if Seamus would make the climb, should he need to. Although they would worry about that later. For now, he took the last couple of large steps to the summit and lifted himself up onto his feet. He looked around slowly fearful of slipping, and turning through three hundred and sixty degrees, stood wide eyed, looking at the most spectacular sight he had ever seen.

It was truly the most fantastic, breath-taking view. He had seen television programmes and pictures in books, but nothing could have prepared him for the magical sight that now surrounded him. He stood transfixed, forgetting about his cold fingers and tight chest, staring at a cloudless landscape on top of the world. A world ablaze in blinding white snow, atop a sea of undulating mountains. And, for a moment, he forgot about the perils of the situation that he and his friends found themselves in.

Taking time to visualise the whole picture and having found no evidence of the figure that Paxton had seen, Reggie's eyes followed the direction of the sun's rays and fixed, in the distance, on a tall and extremely fast flowing waterfall. As it cascaded down, it looked as though it started in heaven and fell into the very soul of the earth and, somehow, he could not take his eyes off it. He watched, captivated, and as the water fell, Reggie felt as if it was speaking to him. Quietly calling his name, beckoning him to come closer. It was still a long way off, yet for a reason he could not explain, he knew they had to head towards it.

Shaking himself back to reality he retraced his steps halfway back towards Seamus, Paxton and Jasmin, and shouted with all his might. "Hey, guys, can you hear me? You have to see this. I have found somewhere we can head towards and hopefully find some shelter, but it means coming up here and over the top. I promise it will be worth it, it looks like a winter wonderland. Just follow the route I took, and I will meet you halfway."

"Thank goodness you're okay. We were getting worried," Paxton called back. "What about Seamus? Will he manage it?"

"Definitely. It's not too steep, just hold his arm and guide him. There are a couple of slippery parts, so take it slowly. Seamus is pretty steady on his feet. He will be fine, and I will meet you in the middle."

Reggie had been right; it was a little slippery and the climb was slow going with the two girls guiding Seamus, one from the front and one from the back. They were happy when they caught up with Reggie who led Seamus to the top. And like their friend before them, they marvelled at the view they witnessed.

"Are you crying, Jas?" Seamus asked his young friend, hearing the gentle sound of a sniffle in his ear.

"Sorry, forgot you could hear me," she replied wiping her wet cheek. "It is so beautiful; I wish you could see it, that's all."

"That's sweet, Jas, but please don't cry. I am here with you guys; we are alive, and I will be able to visualise it from the way you describe it. That is enough for me," he stopped talking for a moment, listening, and then said, "Can I hear flowing water?"

"Yes, Seamus, you can. Crikey, you are amazing! In the distance towards where the sun is shining there is a huge waterfall and I thought if we head in that direction we might find some shelter," Reggie told them, omitting the fact that the waterfall had called to him; not wanting to sound crazy. "It means climbing down the other side, but it looks much flatter from there. Shall we?"

Doing what was quickly becoming second nature for D-vision, they supported and helped each other down the other side of the hill and were pleased to reach the safety of some flat ground below. It pleased them to see how well Seamus coped with the descent and were happy to let him walk for himself for a while. The day was passing, and they had no way of knowing how long they had been walking. Their only hope was that on reaching the waterfall they would find some sort of shelter. They were all hungry and tired, and worse than that, the thought of spending a whole night out in the open of this majestic but freezing white wilderness terrified them.

The sun was still up - although it had dropped lower in the sky - and the children were thankful that it had guided them in the direction they needed to go; shining directly on the water as they moved towards it. When finally, getting close enough to take it in, they were able to see the foot of the waterfall where it cascaded into a crystal-clear, blue lake.

"I don't believe it. Look! There in the water, it looks like someone swimming towards the waterfall," Reggie cried, feeling satisfied that he had finally seen one of Paxton's elusive figures.

"You are right, Reg. There, I see it too," Jasmin yelled jumping up and down. "There is someone in the water."

"They must be mad," Seamus commented. "It must be absolutely freezing."

"Yes, it must be, but there has to be a reason for them to be in the water." Reggie told his friends. "When I first saw the waterfall, I sensed it was calling to me. I felt very drawn to this place for some reason."

As Reggie finished his sentence, he, Paxton and Jasmin watched as the body swam straight into the base of the waterfall and disappeared.

"Did you see that?" Paxton couldn't believe her eyes.

"Sure did. You know what that means, don't you?" Reggie said.

"No," they all replied.

"It means there is something behind that waterfall that we need to see. Maybe a cave or something, where we can get a decent rest away from the elements."

"Really Reg, how are we going to get there? We can't get around the lake. It's too big." Paxton took a second to get her head around what Reggie was getting at. "Oh no, you don't mean. We can't, Reg. We will die of frost-bite."

"Oh yes, I do. We can't stay out here in the open for much longer. The sun will be setting soon, and we have just seen someone swim in it without freezing; so, I reckon it's our only choice."

"It does look inviting, Pax," Jasmin said as she began to remove her boots. "Come on, we just have to keep moving to keep warm. Race you across."

And before Paxton, Reggie or Seamus had time to stop her, Jasmin ran and jumped into the water. She splashed her arms and legs around frantically to try and keep warm. Very quickly the others followed. Reggie removed one of his socks so he could hold one end and Seamus could hold the other, and a moment later all four of them were in the water swimming with all their might.

As they approached the base of the waterfall, Jasmin closed her eyes and swam through first, followed closely behind by Paxton and then the boys. Once through they found themselves in a pool of shallow water that led up a bank and onto dry land.

"Not so bad, was it?" Reggie was glad they had made it across in one piece.

"No, not so bad," Paxton relented, "and look Reggie, you were right."

Directly in front of them, behind the waterfall, stood a large opening in the rock face. The hole was big enough for them to walk through if they lowered their heads slightly, and Reggie warned Seamus to walk with his knees bent. Delighted to have found some shelter they made their way inside. It was dark although surprisingly warm compared to the outside temperature, which pleased them because of their wet clothes. They each removed their soggy coats and moved deeper inside where they were welcomed by a bright light emanating from the back of the cave.

Following the light, they made their way further into the rocky grotto. Suddenly they realised it was not a light at all, but a hole in the rocks just large enough for each of them to crawl through. One by one, they knelt and wriggled their way through. Once on the other side, the four friends found their feet and stood bolt upright. Reggie, Paxton and Jasmin gasped at the vision they found before them.

"Why the gasp? What is it, guys? What can you see?" Seamus demanded to know.

CHAPTER SIX
ENTERING PARADISE

"Hey, come on, what is it? What can you see? I know there is something; don't keep me in suspense," Seamus was anxious to know what was going on.

"You wouldn't believe it, even if you could see it," Reggie told his friend. "Can you feel how warm it is here? The sun is beating down and we are surrounded by ..."

"By what? Spit it out, Reg. A chap could die from the wait."

"What he is trying to say, Seamus, is that we seem to have found ourselves in an entirely different place. The snow has gone, and we are surrounded by trees and shrubs brimming with vibrant coloured flowers," Paxton too found it hard to explain. "The sun is high in the sky; the ground is dry, and it looks like we are in a most beautiful, blossoming, exotic garden."

"Wow! Look at this place, it's amazing." Jasmin, as shocked as the rest of them was suddenly filled with new vigour and excitement. "Come on, let's explore."

Before the others could answer she was off again, this time running through the trees.

Trying to keep up with their eager young friend, Reggie, Seamus and Paxton followed through a jungle of tropical topiary bearing different fruits and berries, and bushes covered in vivid blooms as large as their faces. Their clothes dried quickly in the warm sun and once through the thick of the greenery they met with a gravel path.

"Shush a minute. I think I hear something," Seamus was at it again. "It sounds like voices, children's voices."

Seamus, unknowingly, pointed in the direction the path was leading, so they continued, walking further away from the entrance where they had first emerged. As they walked the voices became louder until Reggie, Paxton and Jasmin could hear them too.

Minutes later the trees ended, and D-vision were once again stunned by what lay before them. They had indeed entered a completely new world. Fields and meadows filled with animals; some the likes of which they had never seen before. Children running around, playing and having fun. Adults going about their own business, all unaware of the strange visitors watching them. There were sheep, ponies and cattle roaming. Meadows overflowing with crops and plants. Scattered, far and near, there were small dwellings made of wood and stone, with willow roofs, giving a village atmosphere. Gentle sounds of chimes blowing in the breeze filled the air and the expanse of this mysterious land spread as far as the children's eyes could see.

Seamus could hear so many different sounds he felt completely muddled, that however, was nothing compared to the confusion that Reggie, Paxton and Jasmin felt.

"Bloody hell!" was all Reggie could find to say.

"What is this place?" Jasmin questioned. "It looks like some sort of magical paradise. How on earth can a place like this be here, amongst the mountain range, hidden behind the waterfall?"

"I know this place. It's mentioned in the book that Sister Alice lent me. A mystical utopia high up in the Himalayan Mountains, hidden away from the rest of the world," Paxton seemed pleased she knew something that no one else did. "Everyone, I think we've found Shangri La. Supposedly, a fictional place first written about in a novel back in the 1930's. It is said to be a harmonious, gentle paradise where the inhabitants live forever and is as close to heaven on earth as you can get."

"You've mentioned it before, Pax," Reggie remembered. "But people that live forever …. Really?"

"Yes, and it is definitely not fictional," Seamus added, "if you really believe that is where we are."

"I said supposedly fictional. There are many that believe it to be a real place and people have been unsuccessfully looking for it for years."

"If no one can find it how come we did?" Jasmin was intrigued by Paxton's story.

"No idea, Jas, but now we're here, let's enjoy it. Come on, let's explore." Paxton took Jasmin's hand and led the way.

As the boys followed the girls further into the strange land, Reggie described to Seamus what he could see. He still found it odd that the people moving around did not seem to notice them, or if they did, they chose to ignore them.

Passing several huts, the D-vision members strolled across a meadow; crossed stepping-stones over a narrow stream and meandered through a large orchard of peach and orange trees. On the other side they were met by three tall buildings that looked like they were made of several giant hats: one placed on top of another. Each with ornate wooden, carved, fret work around the walls and windows, and painted in variations of red and gold. The three large buildings seemed to have been built in a triangular formation and surrounded an enormous, round lake.

The lake was enclosed by a small stone wall that was engraved with carvings of angels and cherubs. The motionless water shone a bright emerald blue-green that made prisms of colour where the sun's rays hit the surface. Either side of the pool stood two towering steel pillars, taller than the three nearby buildings, and the four children listened as a low-pitched whirring sound emanated from them.

"Anyone have any ideas what the poles are for?" Paxton asked.

"Poles. What poles?" Seamus wanted to know.

"There are two metal poles either side of a huge round lake. They must be a hundred feet high. And they are making a weird humming sound," Reggie told him.

"Yes, I hear the noise. I wonder what they do?"

"That, my friend, is a very long story." A strange voice spoke from right behind where the children stood.

All four jumped from the surprise. "What on earth…" Reggie exclaimed as they turned and came face to face with a young man with rosy cheeks and long black hair tied tightly in a plait that hung over his shoulder and down to his waist.

"Good day, visitors. Please forgive the intrusion, I hope I did not frighten you. You are all welcome here, we have been expecting you," the strange young man told them.

"Expecting us? I don't understand," Reggie's shock spoke for all of them. "Who are you and what is this place?"

"Questions. So many questions. All will be answered in good time. My name is Tashi, which in your language means 'fortunate', and I have been sent to greet you. Now Reggie, Seamus, Paxton and Jasmin, if you would care to follow me, you must be hungry and tired from your journey."

"How did he know our names?" Jasmin whispered as they walked behind Tashi.

"God knows, but I don't think we had better ask at this moment Jas, let's just follow him and see what happens. Hopefully, things will become clearer soon," Reggie whispered back.

"Indeed, they will, Reggie," Tashi said without turning his head, continuing to walk.

"Not another one with super hearing?" Reggie's comment made Seamus smile.

"Yes, Reggie, you will discover many super things while you are here," Tashi told him.

He led them into a large wooden building where people sat all around eating and drinking. As they had when the children first arrived, the inhabitants ignored them and went about their meal. The room was set out like a large banqueting hall with long trestle tables overflowing with a feast of fruit, bread and meat.

The friends continued to follow the length of the room and through an archway at the other end, where Tashi showed Reggie, Seamus, Paxton and Jasmin into a large bedroom with four mattresses on the floor covered in fur blankets. It had a stone floor covered with several brightly coloured woollen rugs and slatted shutters covered the glassless windows. It was a plain room yet felt homely in a primitive way.

Suddenly, none of that mattered. D-vision were alive, safe and warm. They did not know how they would find their way home, but for now all they wanted to do was rest. They had been through so much in the last day and a half, and the beds looked very inviting.

"I thought you would prefer your own space, rather than eating with the rest of us. There is a small room to wash yourselves," Tashi told them pointing to a door in one corner of the room. "And we have laid out plenty of food there on the table to satisfy you. I will leave you now, as I understand you must all be very tired from your travels. Please eat, sleep and in the morning all will become clear. Goodnight, my friends, and welcome to Shrin Gala."

CHAPTER SEVEN
DISCOVERING SHRIN GALA

"You thought you were so clever, saying that this place was Shangri La. Well, you were wrong, Pax," Jasmin said as she lay on her bed the following morning.

"Well, I don't think I am wrong. The description of the place is the same. Maybe they just got the name wrong," Paxton defended her theory.

"I'm sure they know the name of their own country. Just admit it, you were wrong."

"Hey, you two, some of us were trying to have a lie in," Reggie sat up in his bed stretching his arms high above his head. "Who was wrong about what?"

"Paxton, still thinks this place is Shangri La. I was just pointing out she's wrong, but she won't admit it.".

"I won't admit it because I'm right." Paxton moved to one of the windows throwing open the shutters and flooding the room with sun light.

"Come on, stop arguing, ladies." Seamus was now awake too and not happy they had woken him up.

"Yeah, Seamus is right, you shouldn't be arguing," Reggie was interrupted by a tap on the door of the large bedroom.

The door opened and Tashi entered, dressed in a red tunic that fell to the floor. "Good morning, dear ones, I thought I heard voices. I trust you slept well and are adequately rested this beautiful morning. Please join us for breakfast in the main hall. You will find fresh clothing for you all in the closet," he said and left the room closing the door behind him.

"Okay, no time for any more arguing, we have our orders. Let's get dressed and have some breakfast. I don't know about you, but I'm starving," Reggie said jumping off his mattress.

"Me too. Some one point me in the direction of the closet please," Seamus requested.

Once dressed in outfits of yellow tunics and cropped trousers, with leather moccasins; the four friends found the dining hall they had walked through the evening before. It seemed as though everyone had already eaten and gone about their business, so they had the enormous room to themselves. There was bread and eggs with fresh juice for them to drink, and when they finished Tashi appeared and apologised for not joining them, saying that he had been attending morning prayers.

"It is a good morning, Reggie, Seamus, Paxton and Jasmin. I hope you enjoyed your breakfast."

"How come you know all our names?" Jasmin was curious.

"I know a lot about you, little one. Your parent's homeland of India covers much of the southern and western aspects of the Himalayas. I hope you have been continuing with your puzzle solving," Tashi surprised her.

"Me. What about me?" Paxton was intrigued.

"We are eternally sorry for how our stepfather treated you but thank the gods he is now out of harm's way. Let's hope nothing here makes you scream," he said with a gentle grin.

"Wow! You are amazing. Do you read minds?"

"Well, as a matter of fact, Jasmin, I can. However, that is a story for later. If you would all be kind enough to come with me, I will introduce you to our home."

Reggie, Seamus, Paxton and Jasmin followed in silence and as they walked, Tashi talked. He explained that his people knew of their plane going down and that the figures they had seen, had been sent to guide them to their destination. The children were shocked by what Tashi told them, also learning that these native strangers had been responsible for the plane being taken over and pulled into the Himalayas - and at no time were they ever in real danger.

"What about Sai and John the pilot, are they dead?" Reggie asked knowing they all wanted to know.

"They are both fine. They were taken to a hospital in Nepal and are on the mend. Now, shall we sit for a while, and I will tell you about life here." Tashi sat down under a cherry blossom tree and a small girl brought them some Chinese tea.

"The people of Shrin Gala are an ancient race called Shrinda and collectively we are known as Shrinians. We are made up of Sana, the youngers and Purana, the elders. Every new baby is brought up by the Purana women, with the aid of the Badg-its, a half badger half rabbit creature, native to our land. The Sana who led you here are free to come and go and visit towns on the outside. On reaching the age of sixteen we become the Purana and must decide whether to stay or leave. If we stay, we stay forever. If we choose to leave, we are forbidden to ever return."

"That seems a little harsh," Jasmin broke into Tashi's story. "Sixteen seems very young to have to make such a big decision."

"Some may say that Jasmin, it is, however, a way of life here. Every Sana is raised to know it is the choice they will have to make, and we are all greatly prepared for the outside world, should we choose it."

"What happens if you decide to stay?" Seamus asked.

"The Purana are split into three groups: the labourers, who are the workers; the servers look after us; and the teachers are the knowledge givers. We are given our group by our governing council when we turn sixteen, and each group has its own temple."

"Are those the three large buildings we saw by the round lake?" Reggie questioned.

"Yes, one for each of the groups. As Purana, we live to the age of one hundred. We then drink the juice from the sacred Nyingchi tree and are laid in the relevant temple of our adult lives and fall into an eternal slumber. Once asleep the soul leaves and is captured in a box which will have been placed next to the sleeping body. When the box is later found to be open and empty, it means the soul has been taken to be used to reincarnate a new body and the old body can be cremated."

"You mentioned a council," Seamus was fascinated and wanted to know more.

"Yes, Seamus, the Tsering council. Tsering means 'lifelong' in English, and it is made up of all the Purana in their hundredth year, with our oldest living Purana, the Kunchen 'all knowing' heading the chair. We have no police or authorities in Shrin Gala as there is no crime, so the Tsering council rule over everything. We live a quiet, happy and simple life, being self-sufficient and supporting ourselves, and living long lives without illness or disease.

"It truly is the most beautiful place I have ever seen, but how can you live without crime and illness, when people come in from the outside world," Jasmin queried.

"It is a beautiful and magical place, completely shut off from the world and no one from the outside comes here."

"How can that be possible?" Reggie wanted to know. "Admittedly it was pretty hard to find, and we were led here but it must be on maps and stuff, and surely it can be seen from the air."

"That is where the magic comes in. Our perimeter is protected by a magnetic force field, and it makes Shrin Gala completely invisible to the outside world. We are never located by aircraft as the polarity here makes compasses spin anticlockwise, out of control, and radar systems go haywire and berserk."

"Is that anything to do with the two tall pillars near the lake? I think I remember something about polarity from physics," Reggie told him.

"Indeed, it is. There is an electromagnetic force between the north and the south posts that conduct an electric current which produces the invisible magnetic field."

"Crikey. That's amazing!" Reggie exclaimed.

"It sure is," Jasmin agreed, "yet it doesn't explain why there is no illness here."

"Reggie, you mentioned remembering a little about polarity. Well, the round lake between the pillars is called the Pool of Polarity. There is a magnetism in the water that restores all organisms. Polarity therapy restores by emotionally and physically balancing the body, preventing stress which can manifest as injury or disease, thus allowing the body to perform a natural healing process. This allows us to be constantly restored and rejuvenated throughout our lives, ensuring we live a healthy existence until we enter our eternal sleep. We also believe that our healthy bodies leave us with healthy souls that are then passed on during the reincarnation process."

"Absolutely incredible," Seamus exclaimed.

"Certainly is," Reggie agreed. "I have never heard anything so fascinating in my whole life."

"Tashi, I have read about a place such as this in a book I was given. The book says it is a fictional place, although many people believe it does exist. But I thought it was called Shangri La."

"Paxton, the word Gala means grand, and Shrin means shrine, and over the centuries rumours of a strange utopian land that no one can find have spread across the world. The name has been misquoted and mispronounced time and time again, and has in recent years become known, quite incorrectly by westerners, as Shangri La. So, you are almost right. Your Shangri La is our grand shrine, Shrin Gala."

"I have just realised something else," Jasmin shouted. "Shangri La is an anagram of Shrin Gala. You were right after all, Pax. It is the same place."

"Yes, indeed, Jasmin. I knew if anyone figured that out, it would be you," Tashi told her. "Now, shall we take some lunch and then I will give you a guided tour."

CHAPTER EIGHT
AN OLD-FASHIONED STORY

Reggie, Seamus, Paxton and Jasmin ate a lunch of fresh fish and salad and chatted about all they had learnt that morning. Paxton was pleased that the place she had talked about to her friends was the very same place where they now found themselves. The others were just amazed that they had made it there at all. They thought about Mother Mary and Sister Alice and wondered if anyone had told them about the plane crash and that they were alive. They feared that it would break Mary if she thought they were dead, and Reggie told himself that he would talk to Tashi about it later.

As if by magic, the moment they finished Tashi appeared and offered them the tour of Shrin Gala he had mentioned earlier that day.

"Are you ready? Shall we proceed?"

The four D-vision members followed Tashi from the main dining hall and started the tour in the nearby fields. They watched some of the labourers milking cows and goats, shearing sheep and grooming ponies. There were some ploughing fields with horse-drawn ploughs and others cutting fruit from the trees and gathering vegetables from the ground. The labourers went about their day and seemed happy in their work.

"What happens if when you turn sixteen, you don't want to be a labourer," Paxton asked.

"You can put your case forward to the Tsering council, asking to be considered for a different role. You must give valid reasons, however, why you would be better suited elsewhere. The council will then make a decision, and their word is final. It rarely happens though, as we are brought up to understand that the role we are allocated is our destiny."

Next, Tashi showed them inside some of the residents' homes. They were small and basic, having everything the Shrinians needed to live comfortably. Each had a small cooking area, and everyone had the choice whether to eat in their own homes or in the main dining hall. The only stipulation was that they all joined together to eat after morning prayers on a Sunday.

They met some of the Purana women tending to new babies and it amazed them to witness the strange creatures called Badg-its, watching over the sleeping infants, ready to alert the women when they awoke.

"They are so sweet," Jasmin said picking one up and hugging it tightly. "How come they are able to do this?"

"It is a very natural instinct to them, Jasmin. As long as there has been a Shrin Gala, there have been Badg-its to watch over the young. We also have Squisels, that work in the fields helping to gather the fruit from the trees."

"Really, what are they?"

"They are half squirrel, half weasel and have an aptitude for accessing the tops of the trees where our labourers find it hard to reach."

"Can we see one, please?" Jasmin asked, putting the Badg-it carefully down on the floor.

"Yes, of course. Let us head to the orchards."

In the orchards they chased and ran among the Squisels, picking apples, peaches, oranges and lemons as they went. The working labourers were polite and said they were glad that the children had come to help them. Reggie picked up on the phrase and wondered what they meant. The girls just seemed to enjoy the freedom of the space and the warmth from the sun.

"This place is so cool," Jasmin beamed. "I love it here, and I love your strange little animals. I would love to take one home with me. Mother Mary would love a Badg-it to help take care of us."

"I am sure she would. Talking of your Mother Mary, a letter has been sent to inform her of your safe arrival here and that you will return home to her as soon as you are able, hopefully insuring she has no further cause to worry," Tashi told them rather matter-of-factly.

"My goodness. How did you know? That was something I was going to speak to you about later. You really do read minds, don't you? As well as having supersonic hearing," Reggie was astounded.

"Let's just say I do have a talent for that sort of thing. Ahh, look we have arrived at our school," Tashi said ushering the four friends inside. Tashi introduced D-vision to the knowledge givers that were conducting lessons. The Sana were happy to see them and would have liked to spend more time with the young visitors, but the teachers were keen to keep order and continue with their tutoring. They did, however, thank the children for coming to their aid as they made their exit.

"What does everyone mean about us helping?" All four of them were curious.

"If you remember, I mentioned that we knew of your plane coming down and had some of our Sana lead the way here. Well, it was all a preordained plan. The powers that we have meant we were in control all the time. The plane was destined to crash - and you were brought here to aid our civilisation," Tashi began to explain.

"You mean you crashed our plane! Frightened the hell out of us! Nearly killed Sai and John just to get us here. Not to mention the pain I'm sure Mary and Sister Alice are going through at home," Reggie was furious. "My God, you'd better have a damn good explanation for all of this."

"I understand your anger, Reggie. Please let me continue."

They reached the edge of the round lake and waited for Tashi to go on with his explanation. Sitting on the small surrounding wall, D-vision listened carefully.

"Some time ago, for reasons we will disclose later, our crops here in Shrin Gala began to fail, leaving us less food to feed ourselves. Some animals died prematurely and some of our people started to show signs of ill health. Colds spread and some of our infants begun contracting childhood illnesses. These are all things that do not happen in Shrin Gala and sadly were a sign that something was seriously wrong.

"I'm sorry for getting angry and that you've had problems," Reggie relented. "Do you have any idea what happened?"

"Yes, indeed we do. There can be only one reason. It seemed that for the first time in our existence, the Pool of Polarity was failing."

"That is terrible!" Seamus stated. "Do you have any idea why?"

"Yes, Seamus, we believe so. However, that is a story for the Tsering council. Please come this way and meet our most important Purana," Tashi said, leading the four D-vision members into one of the three large, hat shaped buildings close to the pool.

Following Tashi's lead, Reggie, Paxton and Jasmin bowed to the group of four men who sat assembled in the large room. Tashi pressed his hands together as if in prayer and requested an audience with his holiness, the Kunchen.

"Please be seated. We were expecting you, our most welcome guests," one of the elderly men spoke, as all five children sat cross-legged on the floor. "We thank you for your presence here and embrace you with grateful and open arms. His holiness, the Kunchen, will join us shortly."

A moment later, from a door at the back of the room, a short man with a bald head and small round glasses entered, wearing a gold, full length robe. He bowed in recognition of the new visitors and took his place, seated between the four other men.

"Welcome, friends, my name is Kalsang, and I am head of the Tsering Council of Shrin Gala. I thank you for being here and wish to tell you why you have been sent to us."

The old man had the most calming and warming manner about him, and the four friends listened carefully. They found him fascinating and were keen to hear what he had to say.

He explained that the children had been brought to Shrin Gala for a very special mission. Learning of the special powers that each of them possessed, the Shrinians believed they were the Special Ones needed to help restore order to their land and save their civilisation. Reggie put his hand politely in the air and waited for the Kunchen to say he may speak.

"Our abilities are not special powers. They are simply silly, odd little things that we can do. There are probably far more worthy and experienced people in the world who could help you.

"On the contrary. Please allow me to tell you a story," the Kunchen replied. "Every hundredth baby that is born to Shrin Gala is born with special powers, just like the powers the four of you possess. Thirty-six years ago, a pair of twins called Norbu – Jewel, and Amir – Leader, were born. Norbu came first; the ninety-ninth child born since the previous Special One. Amir, born twenty minutes later was the hundredth, making him the new Special One. They grew up as all Shrinian children, and Amir developed the ability to see into, and read, other people's minds. He was also able to seek out other Special Ones. As with all Special Ones, Amir was treated very well, yet unfortunately his slightly older brother Norbu, became jealous. Being the older of the twins he always felt that he should have been the Special One. He tormented Amir and treated him very badly. Amir, however, adored his older brother and did everything he could for him. When they were due to turn sixteen Norbu chose to leave Shrin Gala as he always believed he had not been treated fairly and wanted to go out into the world to get away from this isolated land he had grown to hate. He also wanted to get away from the stigma of being the brother of the Special One. Yet Amir did not see it that way. He loved Shrin Gala and would have done anything to stay forever. Sadly, his loyalty to his brother won the internal battle he fought, and on the day of their sixteenth birthday, Norbu left, and Amir followed."

Captivated by the way that the Kunchen told the story the visitors sat motionless as they continued to listen.

"Life in Shrin Gala got back to normal in the years that followed, although Amir was always missed. The Purana and the Tsering council would have preferred him to stay. Sadly, it was not their decision to make."

Reggie raised his hand again, "Please, Your Holiness, I still don't understand what we can do to help?"

"My dear boy, it will all become clear shortly. Tashi, who welcomed you here, is our most senior Sana and is also our current Special One, born almost sixteen years ago. Like Amir before him, he bears the ability to see into others' minds, and communicate through a type of Extra-Sensory Perception. It seems that Amir has been transferring thoughts to Tashi from the outside world, and we have learnt that since he and his brother left Shrin Gala twenty years ago, he and Norbu have had no direct contact with each other. Amir has communicated that when they first left us, Norbu was so enraged that Amir had followed him, he got his younger brother inebriated, buried him in a hole and left him to die. Thankfully, a visiting businessman witnessed what had happened and rescued Amir and raised him as his own. He taught him his business and left him his fortune when he passed away. In the years since, Amir has kept his ear to the ground, always listening for news of his beloved brother, and recently he has heard rumours that over time Norbu has become increasingly vengeful and is obsessed with getting his own back on the Shrinians for his terrible childhood. It seems that he now calls himself the Tamarind King and wants Shrin Gala as his own. That, dear visitors, is why we need your help."

CHAPTER NINE
A FOURTH LETTER

Dear Mary,

I am sorry that I have not been able to deliver this news to you in person. I am still in India looking into the mystery that took Reggie, Seamus, Paxton and Jasmin away from you.

After a thorough investigation, it is with the deepest jubilation, I can tell you that I have received knowledge of the plane's whereabouts and more importantly that the children, Sai and the pilot are all alive. Sai and John Stokes have been transported to a hospital in Nepal and are both making a full recovery and I shall be heading there in a few days to meet them.

The whereabouts, however, of the children is a little more complicated, I'm afraid. We gather that they were led deep into the Himalayan Mountains and that they are being looked after in one of the villages there. The problem we have is that the region is so vast and isolated it can take a considerable amount of time to cover ground, but we have search parties in the area, and I promise you we will find them.

I understand this has been a traumatic time for you and Sister Alice and I admire how well you have handled the situation. I am deeply regretful and will always feel responsible for putting you through such anguish, but rest assured, I will not stop looking and I will bring the children home to you as soon as I am able.

With fond best wishes,
Amir Mohan

"Alice! Alice!" Mary screamed running to the kitchen. "You have to see this. A letter from Amir. The children are alive. The children are alive!"

Alice leapt from the chair where she sat and flung herself into Mary's arms.

"Really! Thank the Lord," she said as the two women began to jump up and down, crying and laughing at the same time.

It had only been five days since the children left, yet it had been the longest five days of their lives. Neither of them had left the house and had barely eaten or slept. The lady who cooked for the children had been in and cooked for them, but neither of them had had the stomach for the food. As each day passed their feeling of despair had deepened and they had never known such agony and heartbreak. Sister Alice had said a hundred prayers, seemingly to no avail, and both women had felt as if they were being tortured.

Suddenly now, it looked as if their prayers had been answered. The children were alive. Mary showed the letter to Alice, and as she began to read, she started to giggle.

"What? What is so funny?" Mary sounded confused.

"I just had a funny thought. Amir saying, he was sorry he could not deliver the letter in person. Well, it's a good job he didn't, we must look a terrible sight. I haven't brushed my hair in days." And suddenly they were both laughing and crying again.

The feeling of relief that came over them was the best feeling in the world, and as Mary put the kettle on to make a celebratory cup of tea she realised for the first time in days, she was actually hungry.

Drinking their tea, the two women talked about the contents of the rest of the letter and wondered where the children were, and if they were safe. They just hoped that wherever they were, they were being well cared for. Mary knew that the four of them would stick together and give each other strength and comfort. Yet being thousands of miles from home, everything would seem alien to them. They discussed the terrible weather conditions the children could be experiencing and hoped they could keep warm. They talked about how frightened they must have been when the plane went down and pondered how they got separated from Sai and John, the pilot. Most of all, Mary and Alice wondered how long it would be until they were found and when they would be home. That would be a wonderful day: a day of great celebration, although only a temporary one, for Mary still had to find new homes for each of them.

Having not given any thought to the jobs she had to carry out while the children were away, now with the good news, Mary felt she might be able to set to work. Still, it was going to be the hardest job she had ever done. She did not want to think about losing her children again, having just got them back. The work could wait until tomorrow. For today, her children were alive and that was all she needed to know.

CHAPTER TEN
THE TAMARIND ARMY

Since the day that Norbu left Shrin Gala, his anger had increased constantly. Initially he had found it difficult to adjust to the outside world. Away from the tranquillity of his upbringing, he had been plagued with terrifying dreams by night and dark visions by day. He would see the faces of two identical baby boys staring up from their crib, and then Amir's teenage face screaming from under the ground. As the time passed, he became used to the way of life he had chosen for himself, although the visions and nightmares never stopped. He never understood what the dreams meant and convinced himself they were just sent to torment him.

Each time he visualised Amir's face, it strengthened Norbu's anger towards his twin for having followed him from Shrin Gala that day. If only he had been able to understand what he saw but Norbu closed off his mind to the visions and shut them out. He was not going to be upset by them. He was glad Amir was dead, although the feelings of being haunted by him lingered into adulthood. As he aged, the anguish weakened, nevertheless Norbu did not. The visions only fuelled his anger and made him more determined to seek revenge on the people living in the peaceful utopia that had raised him.

As an adult Norbu's magnetic personality did seem to attract attention. Wherever he travelled people loved the stories he told about his childhood. He didn't, however, tell of the pleasant, peaceful land he knew. He told of a dark, sinister place that cruelly held children captive from the world. A kingdom of abuse, starvation and degradation. To all who heard the stories, the feeling of horror was enormous, and they felt nothing but great sympathy and admiration for Norbu.

The storytelling had been the start of his followers: men and women wanted to help him, wanting to know about this terrible place and how it could be kept hidden, without the rest of the world learning of the horrors inflicted there. It all seemed so wrong, and each and every individual vowed to help Norbu with whatever he needed to see that the cruelty of this terrible place was stopped.

He set up a base in the lowlands of the Himalayas in the city of Gyangze, and his followers paid handsomely for the privilege of being in his company. He seemed to have cast a spell over them, telling them he needed their loyalty and support and that they must observe the ultimate in patience, for their plan would take many years to come to fruition. And as those years past, he amassed a fortune dealing in anything and everything unlawful he could find. By the time he turned thirty he purchased a large and secure estate, hidden behind impregnable gates. He became more and more reclusive, waiting for the day he could take his revenge. Continuing his work from the inside, sending his followers out into the world to do his bidding, they fulfilled his wishes and followed his every command, and he named them the Tamarind Army.

"This guy sounds like a complete lunatic," Reggie commented, having learnt so much from Kalsang, the Kunchen.

"Indeed, my dear boy, many would think that. Unfortunately, he is a lost soul trying to understand the ways of the world."

"You talked about him getting his revenge. Do you know how he plans to do that?" Paxton wanted to know.

"Well, yes, I believe we do. We know from Amir, that Norbu remembers from his childhood, that the north and south poles work together creating the magnetic field that keeps us hidden from the prying eyes of the world. Tashi has been informed that Norbu has made a small prototype demagnetising machine."

"How does it work?" Seamus asked.

"We think it omits rays of heat that oscillate in a downward spiral, moving in the opposite direction to our own magnetic rays, thus neutralizing them and breaking them down. And as I'm sure that Tashi informed you, without that magnetic field we are no longer kept secret and left open to be discovered by the rest of the world."

"Gosh, how terrible, is that why some of your animals have died?"

"Most assuredly, Jasmin. We believe he must have conducted test flights over the region. While he remembers the waterfall he does not exactly recall our location, although he must have chosen well as the evidence shows our protection was temporarily weakened. If it happens again it will not be just the animals. Our whole existence will be seriously threatened. He must be stopped."

The four visitors looked at each other with worried expressions on their faces. They had only been with these people - in this strange land - for twenty-four hours yet felt sad they were being threatened and understood how distressed they must be feeling. Suddenly without knowing what each other was thinking, it dawned on them that it must have something to do with why they were there.

"Do you have a plan?" Reggie questioned. "I'm kind of scared to ask. Does it involve us?"

"You are a bright young man, and I assume being the oldest you feel responsible for the rest of your friends. That shows great courage, Reggie. I can see that one day you will make a good leader. And yes, you are part of the plan."

The Kuchen explained to D-vision that through his powers to read other people's minds, Amir could also sense others with similar powers and strengths. The four of them had caught his attention when they were born and had been watched from afar ever since. And now Amir believed that they were the ones to help the Shrinda and had sent them to Shrin Gala.

"That is ridiculous. Yes, we have odd things that we can do but they are not special powers," Reggie voiced his opinion.

"Reggie's right," Paxton continued. "We are sorry for your plight, and we would love to help, but I don't see how we can. We do not have special powers, what good would we be?"

Another member of the Tsering council stood, circled the table where he and his colleagues sat, and knelt in front of the children.

"Paxton Day. Remember when you were trapped in the green house? The skill you used to break the glass and make your escape. That is not the sort of thing the average child can do. And the courage you showed against your stepfather. That courage can always be used in battle. And you, Seamus O'Donnell. You have come through the tragedy of losing your parents and the adversity of sight loss, yet neither has held you back. Not to mention that wonderful hearing ability you have. That is a truly special gift."

The children were amazed at what this man was telling them and sat captivated by the sound of his voice. He moved his position on the floor and looked at the remaining two.

"Little Jasmin Dharlia, you too have had to overcome the tragedy of never knowing your parents but have learnt that others can be a worthy substitute and have shown that you are capable of great love. Plus, your high level of intelligence and great brain power are an incredible asset. And lastly, Reggie Davenport, a true leader if ever we saw one. A warrior, yet a true and loyal companion, with a great power of the mind - and when we put our minds to something we can achieve anything. You are all special and we call upon you to help us. Are you with us, D-vision?"

Reggie turned his head and nodded toward Paxton and Jasmin, then lent over to Seamus and gently squeezed his arm in assurance. "Yes, we are with you, aren't we guys?" Reggie's answer was met with a resounding 'yes' from Paxton, Seamus and Jasmin. "But as for our so-called powers, we have no proper experience or training. Things just happen that we have no control over. I don't see how that can help you."

"You say, so-called," the Kunchen spoke again, "yet they are all special abilities and put to the right use can be harnessed and utilised to great effect. And working as a team, we feel sure that we cannot solve this problem without you."

"Okay, so you must have some sort of plan. I guess you had better let us in on it."

"Yes, Reggie. We have explained what is going on, nevertheless the road ahead is unsure. However, now you are here, we are confident things will change for the better. We assume that Norbu's prototype must be the cause of the disruption and any future plans he has must be stopped before our very existence is threatened any further. The only information we have is that somewhere in his city he is looking into demagnetisation techniques and what effect they have on life. And, of course, he must have conducted tests somewhere near Shrin Gala for the Pool of Polarity to have temporarily lost some of its power. Now, I believe that you have taken in enough information for one day and we thank you for your patience. Please take dinner with Tashi and have some time to yourselves. Sleep well and tomorrow we will hatch a plan."

After an early meal, the four visitors took themselves off for a walk and took in more of the delights of the beautiful land that surrounded them. They talked about how evil and unfair Norbu was being after the Shrinians had given him such a wonderful childhood and it amazed them that this terrible situation had been born out of jealousy.

"You know all this made me think about back home - and Moose and Prudence popped into my head," Paxton said.

"Yeah, I wonder how they are doing in their new home and if they know we are missing?"

"No, Seamus, I didn't mean that. I was wondering if they were jealous of us. You know because of what we can do. When they picked on us it was always to do with something strange one of us had done. It sounds a little like Norbu and Amir. I just think it's a shame that jealously can cause so much damage, that's all."

"Very philosophical, Pax, and yes you are probably right," Reggie told her. "Now come on, let's get an early night. A big day, brainstorming tomorrow."

The following morning, after a breakfast of soft-boiled eggs and fresh fruit, Reggie, Seamus, Paxton and Jasmin went off to the schoolhouse and spent some time telling the students what their lives were like in England and all about Mother Mary and Hawthorns. The Sana listened carefully and were disappointed when Tashi arrived to steal them away. As they left they promised the Sana they would return and finish their stories another time and dutifully followed Tashi to the temple where they had met the Tsering council the day before.

They found the council members sitting cross-legged on the floor, and everyone felt pleased by the less formal atmosphere.

"We have decided," the Kunchen began, "that we can only make a partial plan at this stage. We feel that our first step is to identify what Norbu, and his army are intending to do. So, the four of you, accompanied by the Sana will head to the city of Gyangze to track down the army headquarters, infiltrate the building and endeavour to learn exactly what Norbu is planning. You will then return and report back and depending on what you find out, the next step can be planned and put into action."

"Sounds like a solid plan. How will we get there?" Reggie knew it would be a long journey.

"It will not be the easiest of trips and will take many days to travel there and return. You will have money and the guidance of the Sana for part of the journey, and using your skills, initiative and courage we know you will be successful. Tashi will sort appropriate clothing for you, and you will leave tomorrow at dawn. Now, go with the knowledge that we are depending on you all. The Tamarind Army must be stopped at all costs. Good luck, my friends."

CHAPTER ELEVEN
THE BEST LAID PLANS

The following morning the sun was up by five o'clock and so were the children. Tashi explained the length and logistics of the journey and by six o'clock the team were ready to leave. The first part of the journey would take them some fifty kilometres in a south-easterly direction to the village of Namling in Tibet. This would take two days with a stop overnight to camp. A team of Sana would travel with them, carrying the equipment and clothing required, using sledges pulled by a team of dogs. It would be a long and arduous trek, but essential to the plan. Once in Namling, the Sana would leave Reggie, Seamus, Paxton and Jasmin and they would be met by an associate of Amir's from Mohan Industries who would drive them the ninety kilometres to the city of Gyangze.

It was important that the Sana tried to stay hidden as best they could on the journey and did not travel into the town. They were taught to be masters at concealing themselves, so locals did not get used to seeing them: that would lead to questions and that could be detrimental to Shrin Gala.

The trek to Namling was a scary prospect for D-vision, knowing they had to head back out into the white wilderness away from the warm, safe utopia where they had spent the last few days. Nevertheless, that was nothing compared to what might happen once they arrived in Gyangze and attempt their mission; secretly they were terrified and discussed their fears over breakfast. Reggie, as ever the voice of reason, reassured them that by sticking together they could achieve anything: the proud and simple civilisation of Shrin Gala was depending on them.

Once outside of Shrin Gala, the Sana would show them a route around the waterfall and lake, so they did not have to swim, which pleased them, however the rest of the way would prove difficult and tiring. The huskies would pull sledges with their tents, sleeping bags and food. It had been decided that Seamus would ride on one sledge and Paxton and Jasmin would take turns to ride on the other. It would be a long couple of days, but there was no choice.

The Tsering council wished them well as they left, and Tashi had agreed to walk with them as far as the cave. It was nearing his sixteenth birthday and time to make a decision on whether to stay or leave Shrin Gala, so he had a lot of thinking to do while D-vision were away.

"I'm sorry I can't make the journey with you - the Sana will take good care of you. They know the mountains better than anyone. You have nothing to fear in their company."

"We understand, Tashi," Reggie reassured him. "We are sure we will be well looked after."

"You will be, and we shall eagerly await your return. Good luck my friends," he told them. And then the group was gone, through the hole and into the cave.

D-vision and the Sana made their way around a ledge that rested neatly behind the giant waterfall and progressed onto a flattish plain that took them around the perimeter of the lake.

"I wish we had known about this route the first time we came this way," Jasmin commented, "then we wouldn't have had to swim across the lake.

"You and me both," Seamus replied, and the four friends laughed.

As the group made their way further and further, deep into the mountains, it took Reggie, Seamus, Paxton and Jasmin back to the initial walk that had brought them to Shrin Gala. The terrain was heavy going, climbing and descending, up and down, over and over. There were times when the sledges had to be unloaded as they were too heavy for the dogs to pull up steep inclines. The Sana and Reggie carried the heavy loads, while the girls guided Seamus. Luckily, the weather stayed clear and dry and after eight hours of slow travel Rinchen, the oldest Sana of the group, suggested it was time to stop and set up camp for the night before the sun dropped so low behind the mountains and they could no longer see. They had covered half the distance to Namling and needed to get a good night's sleep to arrive in good time the following day to meet their next guide.

The Sana unloaded the equipment, and quickly and efficiently put up the tents while Reggie and the girls looked after the dogs. Reggie and Seamus had one tent, while Paxton and Jasmin shared another. The six Sana shared two tents between them, and for everyone it was beginning to feel like an exciting adventure. The dogs were fed and tied up for the night and the ten members of the expedition enjoyed an evening meal together, as they sat around an open fire and chatted about life in England. Three of the Sana expressed the wish that when their time came to decide on their futures, they would love to explore the world and visit countries like England, whilst the other three found the whole idea disturbing and had no intention of leaving their beloved homeland. The group was evenly split, while the one thing they agreed on and were all sure about, was that Shrin Gala must be saved from the Tamarind Army, and how happy they were that D-vision had come to their aid.

The next day was more of the same; everyone glad of the good night's rest. Feeling refreshed and thankful the weather remained dry, the group continued on their way and by lunchtime the mountains seemed to have dispersed, with the terrain much flatter and the snow underfoot beginning to thin. By late afternoon, the team of ten arrived on the outskirts of Namling, the second largest town in Tibet. The cone shaped hill where Namling stood was four thousand six hundred metres above sea level and nestled snugly at a bend in the Tsangpo River. It was a sparse, barren landscape with little vegetation and was home to five thousand villagers.

"This is where we must part ways, dear friends," Rinchen told Reggie, Seamus, Paxton and Jasmin. "I'm afraid we are unable to travel deeper into the town. We must not bring attention upon ourselves."

"How do we find our guide to the city?" Reggie felt the first signs of nervousness now the time had come for the Sana to leave.

"If you head into the centre of town you will find the Namling Dzong Fort. It is set up on the hill and you cannot fail to spot it. Wait at the foot of the main pathway leading up to the fort, and at sundown you will be met by a man called Kabir Krishna who works at Mohan Industries in Nepal and is a good friend of Amir. He will be in a black, four-wheel drive vehicle, ready to take you the rest of the way. Fear not, my friends, we have faith in you. The Gods have sent you to us for a reason. Now, travel safely and we will meet again when you have news of Norbu's plan."

The Sana vanished with the expertise they used when D-vision first followed them. It was almost dusk, and the sun was beginning to set to the west. The children had been left with back packs filled with food and extra clothing, but the sledges and the dogs went back with the Sana.

For the first time since the plane crash Reggie, Seamus, Paxton and Jasmin were alone again, in a new world they knew nothing about. They watched for a while as people moved around the streets and took in their location. It was a bland looking town, filled with many rectangular, flat-roofed buildings and others that looked like mini temples.

"There!" Jasmin shouted surprising the others, as she pointed to an enormous fort set in the side of the hill. It was a whiteish-grey, stonewashed building with turrets and a red corrugated roof and sat in a dominant position towering over the town.

"What? What is it?" Seamus wanted to know.

"I think Jasmin found the fort. Wow, it's magnificent! Come on, guys, it's still a fair walk and we don't want to be late for our lift," Reggie took Seamus by the arm and led the way.

They arrived at the foot of the hill half an hour later and waiting as promised was the black Land Rover.

"Good evening, you must be Reggie, Seamus, Paxton and Jasmin. I am Kabir," the stranger introduced himself as he stepped out from the driver's seat. "We will be driving through some rough terrain and if the weather is kind to us it will take about seven hours to reach Gyangze. So, I suggest you sleep while I drive, as tomorrow will be a very testing day for you."

And sleep they did. The car was not the most comfortable, yet it was packed with blankets and pillows, and as far as cosiness went, nothing mattered. All four were so exhausted from the two-day trek they could have slept anywhere. When they finally awoke, in the early hours of the following morning, it was still dark,.

"Good morning, sleepy heads, I hope you all managed to get some sleep."

"Oh, my goodness, Kabir, I don't think we realised how tired we were," Paxton spoke for all of them. "I feel quite hungry though."

"If you look under the seat where Reggie is sitting you will find a hamper with provisions inside. Help yourselves."

"Have we arrived?" Reggie asked as he bent forward and pulled the basket forward and opened the lid to reveal the goodies.

"We certainly have. We are just on the outskirts of Gyangze, but I dare not go any further into the city. The car will be too noticeable. It is up to you now. Gyangze is the most prominent town in Tibet and is a very fertile, thriving place. It is home to eight thousand people and is surrounded by a three-kilometre long, red brick wall. We are still at nearly four thousand metres above sea level so you may feel a little dizzy from the altitude if you rush about, so take it gently out there."

"Any idea where we should start?" Seamus felt a knot forming in the pit of his stomach as their mission was about to commence.

"Well, I think you should act as if you are tourists, then you can get away with asking the locals questions. Visiting some of the city sights might be a good start. Perhaps begin with the Palkhor Monastery in the city centre and go from there. Our intel suggests that the Tamarind headquarters is housed close to the centre. I don't think you will have too many problems. Remember of course, they have done their best to keep it secret, so you will have to keep your ears to the ground," Kabir sounded confident.

"No problem there, eh, Seamus?" Reggie said making the group laugh. "How long do we have?"

"The longer you stay, the more chance something could go wrong. We need to have you in and out as quickly as possible. We don't want to risk you having to stay here overnight so I will be waiting here to pick you up at midnight tonight. It is much safer if we move in and out of the city while it is dark. That gives you slightly over twenty hours. Find what you can, without bringing attention to yourselves and do not get caught. I cannot wait for you beyond midnight. Good luck, the Shrinda are counting on you; and remember - don't be late."

Reggie, Paxton and Jasmin watched as the Land Rover pulled away into the darkness and stood looking at each other, knowing their moment had come. It was time for them to work together and prove they were more than just four unusual kids from a foster home in Brighton. D-vision was about to come into its own. They walked a short distance and found a small farm with several outbuildings. There was very little they could do until the sun came up, so they made themselves at home amongst a drove of pigs in one of the barns. Jasmin fell asleep again and Reggie felt a huge sense of responsibility as he watched her. Paxton and Seamus chatted quietly and left Reggie deep in thought, wondering what awaited them.

"You know we are just a group of kids at the end of the day."

"What do you mean, Pax?"

"Well, it just struck me that we have got ourselves into this crazy situation and it is a huge ask for anyone. Sure, we have these odd things we can do, but that can't be enough to fight off an army. Can it?"

Seamus looked concerned, feeling a similar doubt build inside him, now they were about to commence their mission.

"Come on, guys, this is not like you. We can do this. Think of all the garbage Moose used to give us and we always sorted him out," Reggie had heard their conversation.

"Not quite the same thing, Reg."

"I know, Pax, but if we pretend it is and believe in ourselves, I know we can do this."

"Reg is right, Pax, a little faith and a lot of hope. We have to be confident," Seamus knew Reggie had a point.

As the sun began to rise over the city, and Jasmin awoke, the friends gathered up their belongings in order to set off towards their destination. The Palkhor Monastery was easy to find, towering above many of the other buildings. It stood six stories high, set out in a jagged round shape, each storey slightly smaller than the one below, and was crowned by a round turret with a gold dome on top. It was beautifully decorated with ornate artwork that took their breath away. As they looked around, taking in its beauty, locals began to appear close by and started to set up what looked like market stalls. Trucks and horse drawn carriages drew up, dropping off fruit, vegetables, blankets, rugs, pipes and clothes.

"What a stroke of luck! Looks like they are setting up for a street market. That will bring the locals out," Reggie commented, and the children began to mingle amongst the stall holders.

They were surprised by how many of the villagers spoke English, which was going to make their lives much simpler. The girls went in one direction and Reggie led Seamus the opposite way around. They pretended to be on holiday with their school, and the trip to Gyangze was a day excursion. The villagers were very kind and offered them food and gifts to keep as mementos and all the while that Reggie was conversing with them, Seamus listened out for any snippets of information that may be useful.

"Anything?" Paxton asked when they finally met up with the boys at the end of the market.

"Nothing yet, I'm afraid," Seamus told the girls with a tone of disappointment in his voice.

"I'm hungry, can we stop for an early lunch and continue to look again after?"

"Good idea, Jas, although we can't stop for long. We must continue our search soon," Reggie told her, picking her up and giving her a piggyback ride to relieve her legs. "One of the stall holders mentioned an inn nearby where we can get some soup."

They found the tavern quickly and were surprised that the adults did not seem to mind young people being there. It was a bustling place full of men drinking beer, playing cards and chatting noisily. The children stuck to their original story about being on a school trip and enjoyed hot, vegetable soup with warm, freshly baked bread and water to drink. Whilst eating Reggie, Paxton and Jasmin chatted quietly trying not to distract Seamus from listening to every conversation that was going on around them. With the different groups of people, all moving around talking loudly and animatedly, it would have been difficult to pick up anything important. But not for Seamus. His ability was so precise, he could make out every single word spoken by every single person: and it was not long before he heard what they needed.

"Got it!" Seamus whispered. "The group of men in the far corner to my left, are talking about Norbu and his plans. They have mentioned their headquarters and they have made it sound as if it is not far from here. I think they are definitely something to do with the Tamarind Army."

"Good work, Seamus. It looks like they are about to leave. We will have to follow them, and we must be careful not to be seen so we must stay well back. This is it, guys. Are you ready?"

"Yes. Yes. Yes." Came the three whispered replies.

As the group of three men left the inn, D-vision followed behind, pretending to stop and look around as if they were lost. They ducked in and out of doorways and behind walls, so they were not seen, and ten minutes later saw the men disappear through a pair of metal gates that stood around three metres high. Once the street was clear, the children approached the gates and had a good look around, unfortunately unable to locate an easy way in. Whatever was inside was surrounded by a giant brick wall, topped with metal spikes, which Reggie guessed were connected to an electric current. And the entrance gates were solid steel.

"Look! On the gate, a small black box. What do you think that is for?" Paxton was curious.

"I know exactly what that is," Reggie spoke quietly. "I bet it contains a code to open the gate. Jasmin looks like it is time for you to use your talents. Think you can crack it?" he asked as she moved towards the gate.

"I'm sure I can, but I can't seem to get the cover off the front of the box." She had fiddled around with it, and it would not budge. "Reg, I think I need your help."

Reggie stepped forward and stared at the small, black metal box attached to the huge gate. He leant in close and fixed his eyes on the front cover. Seamus, Paxton and Jasmin watched in silence. This was the first time he had ever had to use his mind for such an important task. He had always just been playing around before - now though there was no time for playing.

"Come on, Reg," he said quietly to himself under his breath, and sure enough, seconds later the metal cover on the front of the box slid to one side to reveal a keypad of buttons inside with numbers and letters on.

"Great job," Jasmin congratulated. "Now step aside, it's my turn. Wow, letters and numbers. They really don't want anyone to get in, do they? I would have thought that just a number dial would have been enough."

"Can you do it?"

"Have faith, Seamus. Of course, I can do it. It will just take a minute or two."

"Careful, Jas, your head won't fit through the gate when you get it open," Seamus replied, making them laugh.

"Quiet please, guys. Maestro at work."

Again, silence was observed while Jasmin studied the keypad, and Reggie kept watch. Not every letter of the alphabet had been used on the keypad, obviously for a reason, which made her job easier. She observed how some of the printing had been worn away from certain buttons, meaning they were the ones used. She just had to figure out in what order. Quickly looking at the most used letters she instantly knew the code word, and then just had to add the numbers. Or just one, single number she quickly realised. Not such a difficult code to crack after all, she thought to herself as she pressed the buttons in order,

S P E C I A L 1.

A loud click sounded, and everyone felt their hearts flutter.

"Well done, Jasmin. Fantastic job," Reggie praised. "Just goes to show how much Norbu thinks of himself. Pretty obvious, really."

"That may be so, but why hasn't the gate opened?"

"Interesting. Seamus give me a hand to see if we can push it."

Reggie pushed with all his might and Seamus joined him. It opened an inch then suddenly snapped shut again almost knocking them both over.

"I reckon it is spring loaded, Reg, and it's so heavy I don't think we can push it open enough to pass through."

"I think you are right, Seamus. I will see if I can open it wide enough. Get ready to run through and be quick in case I can't hold it for long."

Reggie stood directly in front of the gates and once again stared with all his might. His body began to shake as if the door was fighting him, but thankfully his mind won the battle, and the gate began to open slightly. He concentrated harder and harder until the gap widened enough allowing Jasmin, Seamus, Paxton and lastly himself, to pass through quickly and silently, entering the Tamarind Army headquarters.

The second Reggie took his eyes of the entrance, the gate slammed shut with a loud bang behind them and the four friends ran to take cover behind some nearby bushes.

"We are in, guys. This is it," Reggie told his friends.

CHAPTER TWELVE
MISSION ACCOMPLISHED

D-vision sat down on the ground behind the shrubs and caught their breaths. Just getting through the gate had been a difficult task in itself, so they knew the next few hours would test them beyond imagination.

Reggie crawled on his hands and knees beyond the bushes to assess the layout of the garden and there, across the beautifully manicured lawns and flower beds, stood the headquarters and home of the Tamarind King and his army. It was a magnificent temple-like structure, built over five floors with slanted roofs cascading down between each level. Like the monastery in the city centre, it was a sight to behold which demonstrated great extravagance and showed that money was plentiful.

There did not seem to be anyone around which pleased Reggie as he reported back to the others.

"The sun will be going down soon so we must think about getting inside as quickly as we can. We can't be late back to Kabir."

"We're ready if you are, Reg," Seamus tried to show the girls that he was confident, and everything would work out all right.

The children kept low to the ground as they moved amongst the shrubbery, until they approached a large, paved area at the side of the building. They waited briefly behind a low wall and were happy they were still alone. Thankfully, there was no sign of any guards which would make their plan easier. As the front gate had been so hard to penetrate, security was obviously not essential.

Reggie ran across the patio to a side door and noticed that once again there was a keycode entry system.

"Jasmin, can you come over? The door has a code on it." And just as she had at the main gate, Jasmin used her skills to decode the lock. This time it was just numbers, and it only took her a few seconds to break it. The door opened and cautiously the four friends entered.

They found themselves in a kitchen and thankfully the place was deserted. Suddenly, Reggie had a moment of panic for the girls. "Pax, Jas, why don't you two hold back in the garden? Seamus and I have got it from here."

"Oh no, you have to be kidding. No way. What if something happens to you? We will never know, and besides, you are the one always saying we are a team," Paxton was adamant.

"Yes, sorry Pax, you are right," Reggie relented feeling bad. "I just worried for a second. I don't want anything to happen to you that's all."

"No need to worry, Reg. We stay together, end of story!"

Having been put firmly in his place Reggie led Seamus and the girls into a long hallway. They passed several doors on either side of the corridor and a flight of stairs heading downwards. Listening carefully as they made their way along, they were still amazed at the lack of activity. The hall was decorated in an opulent manor with Chinese furniture painted in garish, bright colours. Reggie poked his head into a couple of the rooms finding they were still alone, and at the end of the corridor, they ascended an upward staircase, hoping for more success. The first-floor passageway was pretty much identical to the one below, and from where it met with the stairs Seamus stopped in his tracks and indicated to the far end with his hand.

"I can hear them talking. It's a fair way off, maybe one of the rooms at the other end of the corridor. There are several different voices all talking at once but that is not an issue." The four of them settled themselves in an alcove just past the stairs and waited quietly as Seamus listened.

"We're definitely in the right place," he spoke as he listened. "I can identify about six different voices and they are referring to Norbu as King."

"The Tamarind King, the council were right. God, he is so full of himself!" Reggie was angry.

"Shush, Reg, let me listen. The man that seems to be in charge, I'm guessing Norbu, is asking when the machine will be ready. Another man is telling him that it will be ready in the next few days." The others remained quiet as Seamus continued to listen. "The King is saying that the machine will be bigger and ten times more powerful than the prototype, with the capability of destroying a whole community. We know that means Shrin Gala. It sounds like the plan is to somehow manoeuvre it across the mountain range to near where he did the test runs and release it into the air to do its damage. He is talking about blocking off the waterfall and creating a large opening to welcome the world into his new kingdom and using the pool as some sort of therapeutic shrine for healing."

"Okay, Seamus, I think we have heard enough. It's time we were getting out of here. We don't want to outstay our welcome."

"Too late for that I'm afraid, son," a harsh booming voice spoke from outside the alcove.

The four uninvited visitors jumped to turn and find themselves face to face with two enormous men, one waving a handgun in their direction. Too terrified to speak, they walked along the corridor to the room where Seamus had heard the voices, followed by the gun wielding bully and his accomplice.

The door opened and they were ushered inside and pushed down onto a large, soft sofa.

"What have we here then?" a tall man, the children assumed was Norbu, spoke.

"Found them hiding in the hall, King, listening to every word they were," the larger man with the gun answered.

"And what are you doing in my house?" the man, they called King, looked calm as he spoke to them again. D-vision, however, were far from calm as they sat in silence.

"I said, what are you doing in my house?" This time he screamed the words and Jasmin began to cry. "It has not escaped my attention that you must have had help or been sent here by others older and wiser than yourselves, as my house is not the easiest to access. Therefore, I feel sad for you that you have been used as bait, and unfortunately, I must teach you a lesson. Now which of you will tell me what you are doing here before I lose my patience."

Reggie raised his hand into the air and waited for Norbu to say he could speak.

"We are just four school friends visiting Gyangze on a school trip and we dared each other to see if we could climb your wall and get in, that's all."

"Rubbish! That is a lie. No one can get over that wall without being electrocuted. I will not be lied to," he screamed again. "Take them downstairs. And maybe while you are down there you will have time to think about the real reason you are here, so you have an answer next time I ask you."

He waved his hand in the air and turned his back on everyone in the room.

Three of the army comrades pulled D-vision to their feet and ushered them out of the room. The pure terror that ran through each of the children was immense, not knowing where they were going to be taken and what would happen to them. Paxton and Jasmin were both crying now, and Reggie was shaking inside with fury. The men pushed and shoved the children back the way they had come, down one flight of stairs and then down a second flight which they had passed when they first entered the house.

Once at the bottom of the stairs the atmosphere became cool and damp, with little light. As they turned a corner the space opened to reveal a large, square room that contained a smaller room in one corner that they guessed was some sort of dungeon. One of the army members unfastened the door and pushed the four of them inside with unnecessary force. Seamus tripped, fell and cut his knee, but did not speak out from fear of reprisal, and suddenly the four of them found themselves locked in the bleak, stone-walled, windowless cell.

Two of Norbu's men disappeared, leaving one who sat on a chair on the opposite side of the room from the prison, where D-vision were confined and on their own. Left to their own devices, a huge smile appeared over Paxton's face. These henchmen had followed orders yet had made one huge mistake. They had locked the children in a prison cell with a glass door.

Jasmin was not paying attention to Paxton and Reggie, as she sat on the hard, stone floor to attend to Seamus's knee. His trouser leg was ripped but she managed to roll up the fabric and clean the cut with a handkerchief she had in her pocket. Their ruck sacks had been taken away so she had to make do as best she could.

The cell was bare, free of furniture or any amenities, obviously to prevent inmates throwing them through the glass. Reggie suspected though, that it was probably safety glass, maybe even bullet proof. So, no ordinary individuals would be able to escape - however, D-vision were not ordinary individuals. They had Paxton.

"I can here you two sniggering," Seamus spoke up as Jasmin finished tending to his leg. "What is so funny?"

"Well, normally, being locked in here may have caused a problem, but luckily for us the door to the cell is made of glass. I guess they had to let light into this god-awful place somehow."

"Isn't it a good job we didn't leave the girls in the garden then, Reg? Glad you are with us, Pax."

"Yeah, me too. As soon as Wally-chops out there disappears, I will do my thing." Paxton was happier than anyone that she had refused to stay outside.

"What if he doesn't go? Does anyone know what the time is?" Jasmin seemed worried.

"It's dark outside now, so time is ticking along. We can't wait all night. We just have to hope he needs the toilet or a drink at some stage," Reggie replied.

The children sat waiting, chatting quietly to themselves, hoping they could get out of this situation and make it back to meet Kabir in time. They did not even want to think about what they would do if he left without them. And if the man keeping watch did not leave, Paxton would have to work her magic, and they would just have to take their chances against him.

Thankfully that did not happen; about an hour had passed when the man got up from his chair. He looked in at the children and seemed satisfied they were behaving themselves and vanished around the corner towards the stairs.

"Ready, Pax, seems like your time has come." Reggie was excited at the prospect of getting out of this terrible prison and hoped they would make it the rest of the way out of the house from hell.

"What happens when the glass smashes, Reg? You know they are going to hear my scream and come running."

"We will get up those stairs as quickly as we can, hopefully before they realise what has happened and get down here. Once up in the corridor, head for the kitchen and out through the same door we came in. Run straight towards the main gate and leave the rest to me. Girls, make sure you get Seamus out of here and if I should get stuck you must go. Do not wait or come back for me. You must meet Kabir."

"But Reg, no ...." Jasmin began to protest.

"No buts, Jas. Please just do as I ask. I am sure we will all make it out safely, I just need you to know where we stand if something bad happens. Now, Paxton, show us what you are made off."

The four children moved to the back of the cell knowing they may get shards of glass coming towards them, but with no furniture to hide behind they had to take their chances.

"Okay, here goes. I should cover your ears, especially you, Seamus. It will seem deafening to you."

Paxton stood tall and took a few deep breaths to prepare herself. Suddenly the image of being locked in the greenhouse years before came into her head. It was an angry memory and she needed to make everything right. She closed her eyes, opened her mouth and let out the most piercing, high pitched scream that she could muster. The sound rang out for several seconds and suddenly a splintering noise came from the door. It turned into a crack and then another crack and finally, Bang! The glass door exploded into a million pieces, sending fragments flying everywhere.

As the glass tumbled to the floor the children looked at the open gap.

"Go! Go! Go!" Reggie shouted pushing his friends through the newly made hole.

Jasmin ran first, then Seamus led by Paxton and Reggie followed closely behind. Thankfully, they reached the top of the stairs and into the corridor before the sound was heard, but all too suddenly as they neared the kitchen door, three members of the Tamarind Army appeared at the other end of the hall.

"Don't stop, guys, just keep going, I'm right behind you." As Reggie shouted, he closed his mind to the situation and concentrated on the furniture and ornaments they were passing in the hallway. As he ran along each object began to fly into the air, colliding with the men chasing them. Chinese vases, flower arrangements, a picture from the wall and then a console table that toppled just at the appropriate moment. The men were slowed considerably which gave the children time to safely reach the kitchen. As they entered, they noticed their ruck sacks resting on the work surface. They grabbed them and as they reached the door, the men entered, almost upon them.

"Keep going, I will get the door," Reggie shouted to his three friends still in front of him. He fixed his attention on the door ahead of them and it flung open. His mind now in full focus, Reggie turned his thoughts to all the objects in the room. There was a hanging rack above one of the worktops full of saucepans, frying pans, utensils and even knives. Now he had fully opened his mind there was no stopping him. As if by magic everything above their heads flew around the room. A toaster and then a kettle also joined the fun, and suddenly it was pandemonium in the kitchen. The henchmen in pursuit tried to fight off the items. The gadgets, however, had a mind of their own and there was no beating them.

Reggie was the last to leave through the kitchen door and back out into the garden. Without stopping to take breath the four of them continued towards the main gate as Reggie used his power to shut the kitchen door behind him and then turn his attention to the gate ahead. Not one of them looked back to see that the men were no longer behind them. They just kept running. The gate flew wide open as they reached it and once through, it slammed shut behind them with the help of the spring mechanism.

"We did it! Oh my God, we did it," Jasmin shouted. "Reggie, you were fantastic, and so were you, Pax. Those men really got what for. I bet they can't believe what hit them."

All four of the children were breathless and stopped momentarily to compose themselves, when suddenly Reggie fell to the ground, his legs buckling beneath him.

"Reg! What's wrong? Are you all right?" Paxton knelt on the ground to help him, nevertheless he seemed temporarily unable to get up.

"I'm not sure. I've never felt anything like this before. Just give me a minute, I think I must have used so much power it has taken all my energy."

"We get that, Reg, but we are not safe here. Norbu will send more men after us. We must try to get out of here and back to meet Kabir."

"I know, Seamus, you're quite right. Jas, can you guide Seamus, and Pax will you lend me your shoulder to lean on. I think I can get up now. It will be slow, but we must get back to Kabir."

The four friends made the gradual walk back to the outskirts of the city, to where Kabir had first left them. As promised, he was waiting with the car, and the children knew it must have been quite late. As it turned out they had made it back with half an hour to spare and were thankful for the safety of the vehicle. Too exhausted to speak they slept through the night once again and before they knew it, they were back in Namling, where the Sana were waiting with the dogs and sledges to take them back to their short-term home.

As with the outbound journey, it took two full days with an overnight stop to camp. The children spoke very little to the Sana or each other. They were all too tired and just wanted to get back to Shrin Gala where they could recover and report back on the results of their mission.

All four of them rode on the sledges on the second day of the trek. Hardly able to put one foot in front of the other, they were grateful for the relief and when they saw the lake and the waterfall, they knew they were back.

Once behind the waterfall and through the cave, the D-vision members found a new surge of energy, the warmth and the sunshine once again revitalising them. Tashi was there to meet them as they exited the cave and Reggie, Seamus, Paxton and Jasmin were filled with an overwhelming sense of joy and relief. They had survived. They had completed their mission. And although Shrin Gala was only their temporary home, they could not have been happier to be there.

CHAPTER THIRTEEN
DECISIONS, DECISIONS

Tashi dismissed the Sana and escorted Reggie, Seamus, Paxton and Jasmin straight back to their short-term bedroom. He knew they must be exhausted both mentally and physically and had been advised to let them sleep. He tended to the cut on Seamus's leg and then left them to rest. Falling asleep quickly, each dreamt of their newly completed mission, seeing different scenarios of how Norbu might make his move on Shrin Gala. They all slept through the night and woke late the following morning to the sound of the exotic birds singing outside their window.

"Everyone sleep well?"

"Oh, Reggie, I had a terrible dream," Jasmin said. "I dreamt that we were trapped in that awful cell forever. Every time Paxton screamed, the glass cracked, but by the time we got to the door the glass had mended and we were trapped again."

"That's awful, Jas. I had a similar thing. I couldn't hear anything in my dream, so we never learned what Norbu's plan is," Seamus added.

"Seamus, Jasmin, come on. I had a dream too, but we are all back safe and sound. We must not think about it anymore." Reggie told them. "We worked really well together and achieved what we needed to. We should be proud of ourselves. I had always believed that the things we could do were just silly and daft, yet I now realise we were always intended to put them to good use. That is why we were sent here, after all."

"What if we can't fight off the Tamarind Army? I keep coming back to the fact that we are just kids at the end of the day, Reg. Even with our abilities, maybe we can't fight this army."

"I know you are worried, Pax, but we are here for a reason, and we should give it our best shot. How about we report everything back to the council and see what plan they come up with; and we can make a decision then."

"Sure, Reggie, good idea." Paxton seemed reassured.

The children dressed in fresh clothes that had been laid out for them the evening before and made their way to the dining hall. It was now mid-morning, and the room was empty, yet thoughtful as ever, breakfast had been prepared and set out for them. The night before they had been too tired to eat. Now though, having recovered from the excitement and tension of the last few days, they felt very hungry and devoured their brunch.

Tashi appeared to help them clear their plates and told them the Tsering Council had assembled in eagerness to hear what they had to say. They knew the way to the temple by now, all the same, Tashi had been asked to walk with them. When the children entered they found the five council members already seated and made themselves comfortable on the floor.

"We welcome you back, dear children. We do hope you slept well and feel refreshed," Kalsang, the Kunchen spoke warmly. "We have awaited your return with anticipation and hope you may now be able to tell us if you were successful."

Reggie raised his hand and Kalsang nodded his head permitting him to speak.

"We do believe, sir, that we were successful. It was a long and tiring journey, and your Sana and Mr Krishna guided us well. Once in Gyangze we quickly located the headquarters of the Tamarind Army, where Jasmin used her skill to gain access to the building. Once inside Seamus heard every word of what Norbu is planning."

"So, the mission was plain sailing for you all?"

"Not exactly. We were captured and thrown into a dungeon, so Paxton used her power to thankfully enable us to escape, and we could make our get away."

"And you, Reggie?" Another member of the council asked.

"Reggie was incredible. It's thanks to him we got away from Norbu's heavies. He had pots and pans, even furniture flying around the place. If it had not been for him, we would have been caught for sure," Jasmin wanted them to know that Reggie had played his part too.

"Sounds like you all worked together perfectly. You are very special children, and you should be very proud of yourselves. We knew we could count on you," the Kunchen seemed very happy. "Now perhaps, Seamus, you can tell us what you heard."

"I heard several voices. One of them was clearly Norbu as the others referred to him as King. His army are in the process of building another demagnetising machine, much larger and more powerful than the prototype version they have already tried. It will be capable of flying over the mountain range that hides Shrin Gala and will be robust enough to completely destroy your protective field, allowing Norbu and The Tamarind Army to move in and take over."

"And do you know why he plans to do this, Seamus?" Kalsang asked.

"It seems that it is all about revenge. Norbu was always jealous of his brother and the way Amir was treated as the Special One. He feels cheated and hates everything that he left behind when he was sixteen. He seems to have made it his life's mission to take revenge."

"Do you have any idea what he will do when he has destroyed the magnetic field?"

"Yes, I'm afraid so," Seamus continued. "His plan is to block off the source of the waterfall from above and open up the entrance to Shrin Gala, allowing the world in. He proposes to use the Pool of Polarity as a place of healing where people will pay to come and recover from ill health and feel youthful again."

"And what, dare I ask, does he intend to do with the Shrinians that live here?"

"We believe he may kill the existing inhabitants or keep them as prisoners," Seamus felt a lump in his throat as he said the words.

"This is not acceptable," the Kunchen sounded angry for the first time since the children had met him. "He must be stopped."

"It will not be easy," Reggie spoke again. "Norbu is full of hate and incredibly unscrupulous. He does not care about anything as long as he gets Shrin Gala for himself."

"This is terrible news for our kingdom, and it has confirmed our worst fears unfortunately. The four of you have done very well and we are forever in your debt. We thank you for all you have done to help us."

Hearing everything that Seamus had said confirmed the council's suspicions that Norbu had already tried to harm their civilisation and that he was prepared and more than capable of trying again. It was just a matter of when.

"That sounds almost final," Reggie noticed a resigned tone to Kalsang's voice.

"We have asked so much of you already and we do not know how we are going to fight off this threat. We are a loving, peaceful nation and do not have the means to see off Norbu and his army."

"Sounds like you are giving up."

"No, Jasmin, not giving up. Unfortunately, though, we do not know when Norbu is planning his attack, and we do not have the resources to match his. We will do our best to protect ourselves, even so we must face facts, it may be the end of life in Shrin Gala as we know it. Now, I suggest you pack up your belongings and we will have the Sana ready to escort you back to Namling at first light tomorrow: where you can call for help and make your return to England."

"Is that it? You're sending us home?" Reggie was outraged.

"It is not safe here now. You have helped us beyond measure, and we cannot impose on you further. We must try and fight this battle our own way."

"Do you at least have a plan?" Paxton wanted to know.

"It seems not, dear girl. We will consult with each other and our more experienced Purana and decide what we are to do."

Reggie stood from the floor and moved closer to the Kunchen, "Will you please excuse us for a moment, sir? I want to speak to my friends in private."

He walked back to Paxton and Jasmin and indicated to them to stand up. He took Seamus's hand and said, "Everyone, outside now."

Outside they sat on the small wall on the edge of the Pool of Polarity. Reggie pushed his hand into the water and pulled out his wet palm and wiped the water across his face.

"What's the matter, Reg?" Seamus could sense something was wrong.

"I just thought we should have a chat about the situation here. These wonderful people are clearly facing a terrible time in their existence, and I think we can help. I got the feeling that Kalsang wanted to ask us to stay but pride would not let him. I honestly believe that between us we can come up with a plan and aid these people in defending themselves. We have questioned ourselves before, and we have proved that if we work together, we can achieve great things. Obviously, if you want to go, I understand, but I am staying."

"Me too," Seamus said without hesitation.

"Me three."

"And me four," came the responses from the girls. "And by the way, you idiot," Paxton said, "what makes you think we would go without you? We came together. We leave together."

"I was hoping you would say that. Let's head back inside and tell the council."

The Tsering Council were both delighted and flattered that the children had promised to stay until the situation was concluded once and for all. The Kunchen advised them that they would be putting themselves in grave danger, yet gracefully accepted their help. Both parties knew their best chance of making something happen to enable saving their precious utopian existence relied heavily on the four children. That was, after all, why Amir had sent them there. Now all they had to do was put their heads together and come up with the plan of a lifetime.

CHAPTER FOURTEEN
LET THE BATTLE BEGIN

Everyone in Shrin Gala was delighted when they heard the news that D-vision had promised to stay and help fight off the Tamarind Army. They were not so thrilled, however, at the prospect of the fight. They had no weapons of any kind and no experience of fighting. They were such a peace-loving civilisation it seemed unfair that one person would wish to strip that from them - especially as he was one of their own. That was the hardest part to bear.

Everyone was on high alert. Watching, listening, paying special attention to any strange or different thing that occurred. The Shrinians had no way of knowing when the attack would come. Tashi had sent telepathic messages to Amir but unfortunately neither he nor his staff could offer much help. The Shrin Gala residents were on their own and could only do their best to protect themselves. The Kunchen tried to reassure his people that they should have faith. But were D-vision their only hope? Amir had believed in the children enough to send them to

Shrin Gala, and he believed they would know exactly what to do when the time came. So, the Shrinians had to believe it too.

The Tsering Council conversed constantly to come up with a plan, although the lack of information did not make it easy. The only thing they knew for certain was that the huge machine would be transported across the mountain range and once within distance of where Norbu remembered Shrin Gala to be, he would launch it into the sky to do its worst.

The Sana were sent out on patrol at different times each day and night. No one knew the Himalayas as well as they did. They were an excellent first line of defence for when the Tamarind Army finally did approach. Seamus went out with them most days to aid their surveillance, in the hope that he would hear the army long before they reached their destination. At least that way it might give the Shrinians time to prepare before the inevitable happened. And inevitable it was.

The Shrinians knew now, for sure, that it had been the first prototype machine that had affected their health and killed some of the animals which only added to their concern as to how much damage a larger, stronger machine could do. The more they thought about it the more they worried, and they almost began to resign themselves to the fact their fate was sealed.

"They don't seem to have any sort of real plan," Paxton commented one day when Seamus was out on patrol, and she was alone with Reggie and Jasmin.

"I know. I think they are just relying on us to do what we can. The sad part is that if we can't do much, they will just give up," Reggie told the girls.

"Do you think we will be able to do anything, Reg?"

"I hope so, Pax. I really hope so."

The three of them talked at length about what might be coming their way and tried to brainstorm ideas on how they could help. Unfortunately, again and again they came back to the same answer: they did not know. It was going to be a case of wait and see, and hope that when the time came, a plan presented itself. The children understood their individual skills and kept faith that Amir knew what he had been doing by bringing them on board to help.

Reggie, Paxton and Jasmin did not see much of Seamus over the next week other than in the evenings when he returned from his reconnaissance. Reggie had gone out with him a couple of times, and the Sana took such good care of him, it gave Reggie the confidence to stay behind and support the girls and the residents of Shrin Gala. And every evening Seamus was escorted back as the Sana changed their patrol groups. They wanted to make sure he got plenty of rest, believing that when the Tamarind Army finally did show up it would be during day-light hours. The Himalayas was a vast, savage, desolate place and moving about by night would be considered a death sentence. So, one thing in the Shrinians favour was that they were certain that whatever was coming their way was coming in the daytime.

Two days later Seamus was out on patrol again, waiting and listening, when suddenly he heard a faint rumbling noise in the distance. It sounded in his head like a low-pitched humming noise, possibly a motor moving across the snow. He sat listening for a while not wanting to raise an alarm until he was sure, and as the sun went down, he thought he heard voices too. It was all a very long way off, and he struggled to fully comprehend the different sounds. As darkness drew in, the rumbling stopped. Seamus waited for any signs of it starting up again; and when it did not, he alerted the Sana to what he had heard and had them lead him behind the waterfall so he could report back.

The Tsering Council were not pleased at what Seamus had heard but were very pleased that he had heard it. They assumed the noise had stopped as the sun dropped so the army could camp for the night and start up towards Shrin Gala in the morning. This was good news; it would give them time to put their heads together and think. It was suggested that Seamus turn in for the night after his long day out on listening duty. He would be needed bright and early the next morning to ascertain when the noise started up again, although he would not hear of it: there would be no sleeping for him. If the Sana were going back out, he was going with them. He was the only one who had the ability to hear the assassins heading their way, so if sitting and listening was the only way he could help these people then that was what he was going to do - even if it meant staying awake day and night.

Reggie was not happy that his best friend was determined to go back out and wait yet he understood why he needed to do it. He told Seamus that he wanted to go too, but Seamus insisted he stay and look after the girls. He wanted them all to get a good night's sleep as they would be needed soon enough and remembering how Reggie had been short of energy after their mission to Gyangze, Seamus wanted him to rest up now. Resting though, was the last thing on the minds of Reggie, Paxton or Jasmin.

With their friend out in the cold wilderness and knowing that an attack was imminent, the three remaining D-vision members went over and over how they might be able to help. Time was running out and, unfortunately, they kept returning to the same answer - wait and see how the situation panned out.

As the sun came up the following morning everyone was on full alert guessing the day of reckoning had come for the Shrin Gala, and sure enough they were right. Shortly after dawn some Sana came to report that Seamus had heard the rumbling noise start up again and, along with the voices, it was getting louder. Not being as familiar as the Sana with the mountains it was difficult for Seamus to judge how long they had before the Tamarind Army reached them, even so he estimated they were two or three hours away.

Reggie, Paxton, Jasmin, Tashi, a group of Purana and the Tsering Council gathered in the temple and knew they had to decide very quickly what they were going to do.

"It is time," Kalsang the Kunchen spoke quietly. He was such a gentle old man, everyone gathered could see how difficult this was for him. If things did not go their way today, he knew he would be the last leader of this sacred land before it was destroyed forever, and he felt the utmost responsibility for all who lived there. "Please, help me. I am too old to make these decisions for the rest of you. You will be here long after I am gone. You must decide what we are to do, and I will know you have all done your best."

Everyone gathered stood looking from one to another. It was most odd that the Kunchen would hand over control. They were so used to him making the ultimate choices they were rather dumbstruck and lost for words.

Reggie looked around at these helpless, innocent people and knew it was now or never. They were not going to fight, and like a bolt of lightning hitting him, he knew he was about to become a man. He was fourteen years old and felt as though he had more life experience than any of the adults around him. He was here to complete a mission and that was exactly what he was going to do.

"Right, this is how it is going to go. Seamus has been out all night and we know we have a couple of hours before they reach us. Tashi, gather the rest of the Sana who are still here and collect anything you can find that can be used as weapons. Shovels, pitch-forks, picks, knives, kitchen utensils. Anything sharp or heavy that can be used against the men. You will all head out with Paxton, Jasmin and me. Purana, arm yourselves too, as best you can. Follow us out and try and make a blockade on the outside of the cave around the lake and behind the waterfall. Council, get the women together. You must do all you can to block off the entrance in the cave to stop the army getting in. You will be the last line of defence if we fail. Paxton, Jasmin and I will do all we can to stop their machine taking off, but if we can't stop them and it launches successfully, they will storm the cave to gain entry. Then I'm afraid it will be up to the rest of you. Now let's get ready. Good luck, everyone."

Reggie turned and walked out of the temple and the girls ran after him. He was not going to wait to see the reaction of the council, he just hoped he had done enough to shake them in action.

"Oh my God, what was that?" Paxton cried as she caught up with him.

"Wow, Reg, you were amazing. What a hero!" Jasmin hugged him tightly.

"Not a hero yet but keeping my fingers crossed. I'm shaking everywhere. Do you think they listened?"

"Oh yeah, they listened all right. It was just the kick up the backside they needed," Paxton said, and they all laughed.

"Come on, then," came Tashi's voice from behind. "No time for standing around laughing. Let's do this."

While Reggie and the girls waited for Tashi and the Sana to gather all the makeshift weapons they could find, they dressed themselves in warm coats and boots, not knowing how long they would be outside of the balmy haven, waiting for the enemy to arrive. Some of the Sana already out on patrol had reported back that there had been a heavy blizzard the night before, so they were knee deep in fresh snow. Guessing that would hamper the journey of the approaching militia, the group made their way out through the cave, still with time to consider their options.

Once on the outside, Reggie, Paxton and Jasmin were happy to meet up with Seamus. They had really worried about him, especially when they heard about the blizzard. He looked very tired, yet thankfully he was still in good spirits and seemed to be running on pure adrenaline.

The Sana informed Reggie they had done a detailed inspection of the surroundings after the downpour of snow and reckoned it would help them. Many areas of rock face that were visible before were now gleaming bright and white which gave them more options for shelter and hiding. The sky was silver-grey, and the snow was still falling slowly, making visibility almost impossible. That combined with the fierce, wind blowing, would make controlling the flying demagnetizing device extremely awkward. It was hard to know how things were going to play out in the next few hours, however, the weather already seemed to be on the side of the Shrinians.

As the morning wore on everyone became more and more anxious until Seamus advised them that the noise of the machine moving towards them was now so loud in his head that the enemy's arrival was imminent.

The Sana went into panic mode and began rushing around trying to look for places to hide and conceal their weapons. It was a very chaotic scene and suddenly, once again with a moment of clarity, Reggie shouted at everyone to stop and listen to him. He had taken charge with the Council and now it seemed he had to do so again with the Sana. He had given the whole situation an enormous amount of thought over the last few days and knew they were quickly running out of options. Once again, as the moment engulfed him, Reggie knew instantly what he needed everyone to do.

"Right, the Tamarind Army are nearly upon us, and we've had no firm plan up to now, so listen to me and do exactly as I tell you. I have an idea of how we are going to beat Norbu, but we must work together. This may be our only chance. The army will have to bring the device through the centre of the valley. Tashi take the Sana and move to the far side of the gorge - over there, the side with the lowest elevations. The snow is thinner because of wind direction and the sun light that has filtered through. Take your weapons and climb to slightly higher ground to protect yourselves. Screen yourselves as best you can but stay where you can see me."

None of them understood why Reggie was adamant it had to be one side only yet did as they were asked without question. The only thing they had to do now was wait for Reggie's signal, then they knew what to do. He then had Paxton take Seamus back to the ridge that led behind the waterfall for safety.

Seamus had already played his part and now Reggie wanted his best friend out of harm's way. However, as they left, he whispered something in Paxton's ear. Seamus heard of course and grinned realising now what Reggie was planning. It was something that no one would have thought of and could only be carried out by one person. It was an incredible idea.

Suddenly, exposed to the elements in front of the waterfall, Reggie and Jasmin were left alone and afraid.

"How you doin', kiddo?"

"I'm fine, Reg, a bit scared but knowing you are with me makes all the difference. I know with you here we can beat these morons."

"Thanks for the vote of confidence."

"No problem. What do you want me to do?"

"Yeah, and don't forget me. What do you want me to do?" came Tashi's voice from behind them.

"Tashi, I thought you had gone to take cover with the Sana," Reggie was surprised to see him.

"I had, although when I saw Paxton and Seamus heading back towards the waterfall, I thought you might need reinforcements. I don't know what I can do to help, but I am here if you need me."

"Thanks, Tashi. I'm glad you are here. You may just be able to help."

The three isolated friends stood close to each other as Reggie explained to them what he had said to Paxton and what he wanted them to do. Suddenly, as they listened with worried looks on their faces, the ground beneath their feet began to vibrate. Then came the rumbling noise, audible now for all to hear.

"I think this is it, guys, sounds like they are nearly upon us. Time to take cover."

Reggie, Jasmin and Tashi moved to shield themselves behind a nearby rock edge, where they could peer around and see the army approaching. And that is just what they saw. About a hundred men at a quick glance, all dressed in dark coloured snow suits. Not great camouflage was Reggie's first thought. They stood out in total contrast to the gleaming white snow. The men walked in a row by row formation, surrounding a huge electronic vehicle that resembled a giant snow mobile and there, resting on the top of it, was the demagnetizing machine. It was a round machine, at a guess about six or seven metres in diameter and looked like an upside-down metal ice cream cone. On the outside of it the children could see metal rings cascading down the main shell and on the very top a large double propeller.

It was clear to everyone that the extra snow fall had caused an array of problems and the army's movements across the surface were very slow. Many of the men looked tired and did not appear ready for a fight. Perhaps they were so confident in their mission they expected the Shrinians to just hand over their homeland. Obviously they did not expect to come up against D-vision.

"Look, there on top of the vehicle, the guy dressed in the royal blue snow jacket - that is Norbu, I recognise him from the headquarters in Gyangze. Tashi, can you get in his head and tell us what he is thinking?" Reggie asked.

"I should be able to. As Amir's twin they are connected mentally, so it shouldn't be too much of a problem. Give me a moment."

Tashi looked straight in the direction of Norbu and closed his eyes. At that moment Norbu rubbed his head and Reggie wondered if he could sense something. Then Norbu put his hand into the air, and the procession stopped.

CHAPTER FIFTEEN
SAVING SHRIN GALA

The children watched as the giant snow mobile came to a halt and stopped rumbling. The Tamarind Army members gathered around as if waiting for instructions from their King. There was a ghostly silence across the terrain as every Shrinian watched from their hiding place. Not even the falling snowflakes could be heard.

"Norbu is thinking that he recognises where he is - that is why he stopped," Tashi spoke as he opened his eyes. "It seems he did not come here when the prototype was flown over. It was a much smaller and lighter model, so it flew in from further afield and now coming face to face, once again, with the waterfall has brought back all his childhood memories. He does not want to risk moving any closer and proposes to launch the demagnetizer from here. He is a little worried about the high winds so wants to complete the mission sooner rather than later."

"Good work, Tashi. You were right about being able to help, thanks for coming back." Reggie knew that as things stood, everything

154

so far had worked in their favour and now was their moment: the reason he and his three best friends had been called to this remote land. It was now that D-vision would prove their worth.

"Okay, Jasmin, are you ready?" Reggie asked the youngest member of their gang who he cared for deeply. "As soon as I give the signal, you move as quickly as you can to the back of the vehicle, and I will have you covered from here. Get in and out as fast as you can and don't put yourself in danger. If you can't find anything, it does not matter just get out, but you must be quick. I don't know how much energy I will have. Are you ready?"

"Terrified, but ready as I will ever be. Let's do this thing," Jasmin was shaking as she spoke.

"Now, you can see they are all concentrating on what Norbu is telling them - that will buy you a little time. And remember, Jas, I've got your back. Good luck, you've got this."

"Good luck to you too, Reg. Look after him, Tashi, he is very important to me," she said, and was gone.

Staying close to the ground and wearing a white coat Jasmin was well camouflaged in the falling snow. She knew exactly what she needed to do. As she approached a secluded spot near the back of the vehicle she waited for her signal. Suddenly she heard the cry of a wolf, which she knew was coming from Reggie. A second later the Sana appeared out of nowhere on the far side of the pass holding their weapons. Reggie stepped out from behind the shelter of the rock and stared across at his compatriots. This was going to take every fibre of his will power, even so he knew he could do it. He had to. As he closed his eyes each item, tool and utensil began to fly from the hands of the Sana directly towards the army.

Jasmin knew this distraction was her cue and charged quickly to the back of the motorised trailer and climbed up. Taken by such surprise, the men did not know what hit them. Not only was the snow impeding their vision, now they were also being attacked by countless flying objects. There was shouting and crying as they tried to scatter from the area. There were screams of pain as some were hit by knives and sharp objects. The scene was chaos. Norbu called out to his men to try to calm and control the situation, but to no avail, as many of them fled. Some were left injured. The worst hit lay dying on the freezing snow. It was a sight that no one, especially a child, should ever witness. Nevertheless, it created the diversion that allowed Jasmin to explore and find what she was looking for.

Thankfully, with all the disruption, she had gone unnoticed and there at the base of the enormous cone device was a control panel. Reggie had guessed that to fly the machine into the air it would need to be operated from the ground and was probably controlled remotely. He had been right, and looking at it, Jasmin knew it was going to be a pretty easy job to disarm it. The control panel was lit with a digital clock which she knew would be used when the machine went up. There was also a small pad with numbers and letters like the one on the gate of the army headquarters in Gyangze. Could it really be that simple? Could Norbu have used the very same code? Only one way to find out. Jasmin typed S P E C I A L 1 into the keypad and sure enough the front panel popped open. She quickly removed a small pair of nail clippers from her coat pocket and looked inside the device at the mixture of four different coloured wires. She had never done anything like this before and had seen movies on the television where great thought and care was given as to which wire to cut. Sadly, Jasmin did not have the luxury of time to decide, so she took the clippers and quickly cut through all four wires, one after the other. Immediately the machine stopped humming and the numbers on the front dial diminished to nothing. She had done what she needed to. She had played her part in the plan. There was no way this machine was being launched today. All she had to do now was climb down and get back to Reggie and Tashi.

As Reggie saw her reappear at the back of the trailer he let out another loud wolf cry signalling the Sana to set free their second round of ammunition. Again, using every ounce of his power, he controlled the objects to fly towards, hit and disable the men. Unfortunately for Jasmin, Norbu saw her too and launched himself from the front of the trailer where he had been cowering to shield himself from the flying objects. He caught hold of Jasmin's leg as she was about to climb down. A moment of panic spread over her as she began to wriggle and kick him with all her might. Luckily for her, Reggie was watching every move and fixing on one specific object moving through the air, he directed it straight towards Norbu. The Tamarind King let out the most penetrating scream as the heavy, carbon steel axe landed in the centre of his back, right between his shoulder blades. His grip on Jasmin released as his limp body fell to the edge of the trailer and then off the side, down onto the snow and ice below where it came to rest in a large pool of blood.

In a moment of enlightenment, as Norbu lay on the frozen ground waiting for death to come, he once again saw the faces of the twins that had haunted him his whole life. Only now, for the first time, the vision became complete. Norbu saw two Purana women arguing over the crib of the newly born boys, both frantic that the other had not marked the babies. It was a chaotic scene. Which baby had been born first? Which baby was the Special One? Neither knew and they made a choice. A secret they would take to the grave.

As the last few breaths escaped from Norbu's lips, he wondered maybe, if he had been the Special One after all. He certainly had the powers; or maybe that was something natural that identical twins possessed. If only he had known the truth, things could have been so different, he thought, as the last breath left him, and his world turned black.

While the confusion of the flying objects continued, Jasmin, now free, jumped from the trailer and made a hare-like dash back to her friends.

"You did it, Jasmin, we knew you could," Tashi congratulated her as they noticed Reggie beginning to weaken. His legs wobbled and both Tashi and Jasmin took an arm each to support him.

"Do you feel all right, Reggie?" Jasmin remembered how weak he had become in Gyangze and it worried her.

"Yes, Jas, I'm fine. Let's get back to Paxton and Seamus and finish this once and for all."

Each with an arm wrapped around their shoulders, Jasmin and Tashi helped Reggie back towards the ridge that led to the back of the waterfall, and as they walked Reggie stopped and let out one last yelping howl. Paxton heard the third cry and saw them approach. Knowing they were out of harm's way, and that the Sana were safe on the other side of the gully, she knew her time had come. She was the last one of these four special children to play their part, and she played it superbly. She told Seamus to cover his ears, took the deepest breath she could muster and let rip with the longest, most high-frequency scream that the Himalayas had ever heard. The sound seemed to last an eternity as it ripped through the mountain range, bouncing off the rocks, echoing over and over. It took a few seconds for the effects to begin but when they did the result was devastating.

First there was a crackle and then a rumble which very quickly turned into a roar a hundred times louder than a crash of thunder. Hearing the sound, the remaining army members on the ground turned and looked up at the mountain to their side. Realising what was coming they tried to flee - unfortunately, there was nowhere to run. As the snow cascaded down the side of the mountain it gathered pace. Tumbling and forming boulders, creating the most frightening avalanche anyone would ever see. The noise was deafening and the sight superb in a spine-chilling way. The men on the ground were petrified knowing that within seconds the end would be upon them. They had come here, following their leader to create a new world for themselves .... yet now their leader was dead and at any moment they would be too.

The children watched as the snow crashed down to the bottom of the ravine, crushing anything in its path. It had no mercy as it covered everything in sight. The noise continued to rumble on for several minutes until suddenly it was over. There was no more snow left to fall, and within moments an eery calm came over the whole area. The flakes stopped falling from the sky and the sun began to shine through the clouds.

Reggie, Paxton, Jasmin, Seamus and Tashi waited in silence, almost unable to move. Seamus took his fingers from his ears sensing that the noise had abated and, slowly, the events of the last hour sunk in.

"You did it! You really did it!" Tashi was the first to speak.

"We did, didn't we? Guys, you were all incredible, especially you, Jas. My God, you were so brave," Reggie was in awe of his young friend.

"We could never have done it without you, Reg. You have been our rock since we arrived here, and you certainly did have my back. Did you see that axe pummel Norbu? Poor guy never stood a chance."

"Poor guy nothing!" Paxton chipped in. "He deserved everything he got."

"Well, I don't know about you lot, but I'm exhausted, my brain is totally fried," Reggie said with all his energy gone. "It's been one hell of a day. Let's get the Sana back to their home and spread the good news."

Tashi signalled to the Sana to make their way back to the ridge, and together they all walked back to meet the waiting Purana. Behind the waterfall they had heard the noise but had been unable to see what was happening and were too scared to move to look. Ecstatic at the news they followed D-vision, Tashi and the Sana back through the cave.

It took a while for the Sana to break through the defence that had been laid at the entrance to their land, and when the remaining Shrinians heard the children, they began to clear the blockage from their side too. Soon enough the hole was open, and every person returned to the safety and security of their home.

The Tsering Council were overcome by the news, as was every single Shrinian. It was the happiest day in their solitary existence: a day that would be marked for ever more as D-vision Day. This group of four young people had been sent to them when their lives depended on it and they had come through with flying colours. They were hailed national heroes. The Shrinians owed them so much and knew they would never be able to repay them for all their invaluable help.

A day of celebration followed with eating, drinking and dancing. The sun shone down, the harvest was full and if ever anyone from the outside world was to find this place, they would not believe their eyes. For now, though, thanks to D-vision, that would never happen. The inhabitants of Shrin Gala could return to their content, simple and peaceful lives.

Later that evening as the partying ended, Reggie, Seamus, Paxton and Jasmin said their goodbyes, knowing that early the following morning the Sana would, for the last time, escort them on the long trip back to Namling to make their journey home. It was an emotional time for all and many of the Sana wished they would stay. However, everyone knew they had their own lives to live, and that Mary and Alice were waiting for them.

"I have an announcement to make," Tashi spoke just before everyone took themselves off to bed. "It is my sixteenth birthday in one week, and I have come to a very important decision. I have thought long and hard, and the last few weeks have shown me that there is a whole new world out there for me to explore. These wonderful visitors of ours have inspired me, so I have been transferring thoughts with Amir and have decided to take a position at Mohan Industries. Amir says he can really use a young man with my special expertise. Sai is going to show me the ropes and Amir is hoping to pass some of the responsibility of his empire to me. Therefore, I will be leaving Shrin Gala in the morning. It has been the hardest decision to make but I know it is the right one for me. I am grateful to you for my childhood here and will miss you all from the bottom of my heart."

The announcement took everyone by surprise, even so they were all happy for Tashi. It was the way of life in Shrin Gala and the Sana's choice to make. Tashi said his goodbyes to everyone and went to his chambers to prepare for the long walk with D-vision the next morning.

After the festivities there was not one person that did not sleep well. They were safe and could now relax and get their lives back on track.

The following morning Reggie, Seamus, Paxton, Jasmin and Tashi had hoped to disappear early without any fuss, but the Tsering Council had other ideas. Every Shrinian had woken early to see them off and wish them well on their journey. They were so grateful and would miss these wonderful young people that they owed their lives to. Music played and some of the Sana sang a song of thanks as the five youngsters walked to the cave entrance. They would be escorted to Namling by a group of other Sana, as they had been when they made their initial walk to find Shrin Gala two and a half weeks before. And now, as Tashi handed over the reins of being head Sana to Rinchen, he felt lucky that he would always have the privilege of having been a Special One. It was an honour that would stay with him forever and be used wisely just as Amir had done before him. He knew that whatever happened or wherever he went throughout the rest of his life, he would love and defend his homeland.

The final hugs, bows, kisses and handshakes were exchanged and then D-vision and Tashi were gone. Back into the cave to set out, one last time, into the expanse of the world's largest mountain range and make their journey onto the next phase of their lives.

Over the next few days, once the weather had calmed, the Sana were sent out to dispose of any bodies that became visible when the snow began to melt. And, slowly but surely, they dismantled the awful machine that had threatened their very being, along with the vehicle it arrived on. It was a difficult task and when completed there was no evidence left of the battle that had ensued. The fight was over. Norbu was dead and Shrin Gala had been saved. Now they could go about living their lives as if nothing had happened. And in years to come as new Shrinians were born, they would not understand what an honour it had been to meet four such astonishing children; whilst they would know how they had saved their homeland, for it was a story that would be remembered and told forever.

CHAPTER SIXTEEN
THE HOME COMING

Summer was over, and Mary had begun to feel in recent weeks that her life was over too. She had received the occasional telephone call from Amir to assure her that everything was still being done to find the children and bring them home. Nonetheless, as time passed, she became less and less confident that she would ever see them again.

She woke on the morning of September 30th, the day of Susan's funeral, filled with dread at having to attend. She thought back to the last time she had seen Susan and the vision of the plane crash she'd had as she drove home. Mary knew now that it had been the start of a terrible few months and the thought of making the drive to South London, this one last time, terrified her. Of course, Alice had hoped to go with her, but unfortunately for them both, she had gone down with a heavy cold a couple of days before. Alice did not feel well enough to make the journey and believed it would be unfair to inflict her germs on the other mourners.

164

Mary dressed in her familiar black dress, the original one she had bought for Mrs Hawthorn's funeral years before and took the drive up the M23 on her own. She arrived at Sutton Crematorium with half an hour to spare before the service and quietly took some time to look at the beautiful memorial flower arrangements that had been placed there.

She met briefly with Mr and Mrs Sanderson and again conveyed her condolences and offered her apologies that she was unable to stay for the wake after the ceremony but would still be willing to say a few words about Susan in the chapel which, of course, they were grateful for.

It was a tender, loving service and reminded Mary what a sweet person Susan had been and how sad it was that she had been taken so young. The eulogy she gave was well received and even made the congregation laugh, thanks to tales of the antics the two girls had got up to at university. It had been a fitting send off for her best and only friend, although for Mary the day had been extra tough due to what she and Alice were going through at home. As she left the cemetery, having seen her friend cremated she had never felt so low. To Mary the whole day had summed up the last three weeks and she felt that she had, in her own way, said goodbye to her four, much loved, remaining children. And now she had the long drive home.

∧∧∧

Alice had been lying on her bed, concentrating on trying to breath when the doorbell rang. She had only just heard it over the sound of her radio. She put her warm dressing gown over her pyjamas and slowly walked down the stairs, holding tightly to the rail from fear of feeling dizzy and falling.

As she opened the door, her first thought was that the medicine she was taking was playing tricks with her mind.

"Hello, Sister Alice," the young man standing in front of her said.

"Oh, my Heavenly Father above. Is that you, Reggie?"

"Sure is. God it's good to see you."

"Hi, Alice, we're home," came that rest of the voices standing behind him.

Alice let out a gentle scream, and as she collapsed to the floor, she began to sob tears of joy. A large hand reached down towards her and as she looked up, she saw Amir looking into her eyes. "I've found them, Alice. I've brought them home. Is Mary here?"

Amir carefully helped Alice to her feet, and he could see that she was overcome with emotion. "I can't believe it. It is really true? You are all home. Praise the Lord. This is a joyous day."

Still feeling slightly weak, Amir helped her into the lounge followed by the children. She explained that Mary was out for the day attending Susan's funeral and the only reason she was there was because she had been too ill to go.

"I have an idea," Amir told them all. "When Mary gets back let me go to the door to greet her. I will then bring her in here to see you all and if the shock doesn't kill her it will be a wonderful surprise. Do you know how long she will be, Alice?"

"The service was at three o'clock so with traffic I'm guessing we should expect her about six."

"Good. That will give you kids time to take a shower and tidy yourselves up and I will pop in the kitchen to prepare some supper for us all. Now off you go, guys. Alice and I will hit the kitchen."

∧∧∧

The drive home this time had been an uneventful one with the exception of the rush hour traffic Mary experienced as she hit the town centre. She parked her car just outside Hawthorns and walked sombrely up the garden path. It had been a very tough day. She hoped Alice was feeling better but did not have the energy to make conversation so decided to take herself straight to bed. She did not feel hungry as was often the case these days. So, there was no need to even think about making something to eat for herself.

She placed her key in the keyhole and turned it. As she did so she felt the door pull away from her without the need to push it. It opened wide and there waiting on the other side was Amir. He was the last person she expected to see. Why was he there? Then it hit her. There was only one reason he would have come in person, and she knew it was not good news. Knots tied in her stomach and a lump formed in the back of her throat as she looked at him. It was the first time she had seen him since he came to tell her the children were missing. So, seeing him here now confirmed her worst fears. He would only have come so far to tell her that something awful had happened to the children.

She flew into his arms, more for support than anything else, and without looking at his face, she whispered through tears that had now started to fall. "I can imagine why you are here. I don't want to hear it, but I know I have to. Oh God, this is so unfair….. Tell me, I can take it."

Amir gently pulled her head away from his chest to look straight into her eyes. "It's all right, Mary. Come with me I have something to show you."

He held her tightly, giving support, as he led her along the hall. He slowly opened the door to the lounge and as he pushed it back it took a second for Mary to register through her blurry eyes. And then she saw them. All four of them, sitting on the sofa talking to Alice.

As they saw her, they stood up quickly and charged at her, squeezing her so tightly she could barely breathe. Suddenly everyone in the room was crying and laughing and hugging each other. It was a moment of ecstasy for all of them and a moment they never wanted to forget. The elation that spread over them was impossible to compare; every emotion of love, longing, fear and joy all coming together at once.

When they managed to pull themselves apart they all sat down on the sofa, squashing next to one another, not wanting to let each other go. Amir excused himself thoughtfully from the room to give Mary and Alice a few moments alone with the children and returned to the kitchen to make a pot of tea.

There was so much they all needed to say but there would be plenty of time for that over the next few days. They were just happy to be back together where they belonged. They drank their tea when Amir returned to the room and within minutes they were happily making conversation as if they had never been away. It was the most heart-warming scene that Mary had ever experienced.

A short time later the children made their way up to their rooms, exhausted from the flight and everything that had happened prior to their return. Alice excused herself and returned to her sick bed, ready for a good night's sleep, leaving Mary and Amir alone.

He wanted and needed to tell her everything that had happened over the last three weeks and how sorry he was to have put her through the most traumatic ordeal of her life. Nevertheless, how necessary it had been to save his people. Mary felt herself falling into a daze while she listened to what Amir was telling her. Every word seemed to pale into insignificance. She had her children back and that was all that mattered. She was not even angry at what Amir had put her through. She had always known that the children were very special, and she was incredibly proud at what they had achieved together to save Shrin Gala. Now they were back, and no one was going to separate them again. The bank could take their home. It did not matter anymore. She knew that they could live anywhere, as long as they were together. They were hers and she loved them beyond all else.

What a bittersweet day it had turned out to be. It had started out very sad and had ended up being the happiest day of her life.

As Mary lay in her bed that night thinking about all that had happened she made a promise to herself knowing that as soon as she got up the next day she was going to contact the authorities to begin proceedings to adopt Reggie, Seamus, Paxton and Jasmin, and make them legally hers once and for all.

EPILOGUE
THE LAST LETTER

Dear Miss Bridges,

It is with great pleasure that I write to inform you that we have, today, received funds in full and final settlement on your business loan with the Bank of Brighton.

As well as the settlement, we have been instructed that, every month a substantial allowance will be credited to your personal account to provide you with funds to keep your home running for the foreseeable future.

We are delighted to be able to give you this news and thank you for continuing to bank with us.

With best regards,

Mr Pennygrabber
Assistant Manager, Bank of Brighton

Mary read the letter with more delight than she had ever known. Her children had returned to her safely and now their future lives with her were secure. She knew from deep within who had paid off the loan and resolved to thank him and tell the children later.

She looked from the window across the garden and watched as Amir played cricket with the children. There was no bolt of lightning or cupids flying over her head yet for the first time she felt that if she opened her heart she could love someone else, as much as she loved her children.

As for Reggie, Seamus, Paxton and Jasmin, they played blissfully with the father figure that had entered their lives just a couple of months before. They had welcomed him into their home and never wanted him to leave. He had already given them a wonderful experience, yet they believed that the adventure of a lifetime was still to come.

End.

ᴧᴧᴧ

∧Λ∧

ACKNOWLEDGEMENTS

As ever a big thank you to my family and friends for putting up with my constant ramblings about plots and characters.

To Peter Barber for being the first brave soul to read this work.

To Sue Boyd-Wallis for being the most amazing proof-reader and for all her invaluable help.

To Claudia Kirkby for the design of the incredible cover artwork.

And lastly, to Lloyd Bonson, my publisher, for formatting the cover and for once again having faith in my ability and bringing this book into the world.

I thank you all. Sam x

∧Λ∧

^∧^

ABOUT THE AUTHOR

Sam lives in Essex with her husband, two grown-up sons and four cats.

She has been writing for many years, although only recently switched genre to write for children. In her writing, she aims to encourage learning through fiction, combined with real-life subjects, people and places.

In her spare time, she enjoys training in the gym and practicing yoga; however, nothing gives her greater pleasure than dreaming up a new plot and putting pen to paper.

^∧^

∧**∧**∧

ALSO AVAILABLE BY THE AUTHOR

Sophie Spirit and the Batting Manor Mystery

Sophie Spirit, a deaf girl of unusual appearance, due to a rare medical condition, has spent her whole young life in London.

Unexpectedly, she finds herself living in a country village where she meets Humphrey, son of Lord and Lady Beaumont. It quickly becomes apparent that Humphrey will not be the only child she meets, when she is visited by three spirits who, when alive, were the children of the Beaumont's ancestors.

Strange things begin to happen, and all too soon Sophie finds herself entangled in a scary and devilish plot to strip the Beaumont's of the only life they have ever known.

Join Sophie as she experiences spooky, unnatural goings on and seeks to help Humphrey and his family combat the evil working against them ....

FORTHCOMING BY THE AUTHOR

The next two titles in the Sophie Spirit series:

Sophie Spirit and the Tower of London Treasure – release 2022

Sophie Spirit and the Perilous Plot at Chedham High – release 2023

∧**∧**∧